bandon

All

ope

---

DICK DENNY

The road to Hell is paved with good intentions...

Foundations Book Publishing
Brandon, MS 39047
www.foundationsbooks.net

Abandon All Hope
By: Dick Denny

Cover by: Dawné Dominique
Edited by: Steve Soderquist
Copyright 2021© Dick Denny

Published in the United States of America
Worldwide Electronic & Digital Rights
Worldwide English Language Print Rights

ISBN-978-1-64583-040-5

Acknowledgements

To the fellas of Bravo Company 1/505 PIR, but especially Mike Piscopo... I would have been a good paratrooper. To Brendan Hoffman... Bro what don't I owe you? And Phil the Destroyer... For practicing like me.

Table of Contents

Prologue: My Way

...the end is here...

It is without any hint of hyperbole or irony when I say Frank Sinatra had one of the greatest voices of all time. Even through the small speakers of my iPhone there was no mistaking the tone and timbre of Ole Blue Eyes himself. I had asked Gretchen to pick a song, a song for the End.

When I say the End, again, it is without hyperbole or irony. The grass was soft and well manicured under my sneakered feet. The wind was enough to tug at the edges of my jacket, exposing the pearl grips of the 1911 under my right arm and the wooden grips of the 1911 under my left. Even with the wind it was a pleasant evening, and probably the last.

Frank sang about living a full life and all.

Gretchen stood next to me, and even here at the End, she was a comfort. I wished she'd go but I knew she wouldn't. I was certain dying was easy. Dying was easy and dying fighting was *blood simple*. It would be so much easier if she weren't there.

But dang it, Frank did it his way.

Then again, it wasn't like she was safe elsewhere. This wasn't just a climax, it was the Climax. She would be no safer up on the International Space Station than she was right next to me. And at least here, she could die swinging. We could die together.

Frank may have had regrets, but doesn't everyone?

I wished Jammer and Switch were here. Switch was gone because I had sent him away, but he definitely would have had I called him. That's the damnation of having Brothers. Jammer was still dead.

Frank sang about doing what he had to do; preaching to the choir brother.

How many people had I killed since the entire shit show had been dumped on my lap? How many bodies had I stacked like cordwood in the name of putting off exactly what I found myself surrounded by?

Frank had a plan and did it his way.

Well, unlike Frank, I couldn't say that about planning. Planning was never my strong suit. Maybe if it was we wouldn't have found ourselves here at the End of All Things.

Frank sang about being in over his head but sucking it up like a man.

Gretchen had to know.

Frank Sinatra sang of standing and bearing it.

That I had, though I'm not sure it was a virtue. I'm not sure anything was better. I wasn't sure anything could be worse. Hell on one side, Heaven on the other, and neither pleased to see us.

Frank sang about loving, laughing, crying.

I kind of wish I'd cried but I hadn't. I hadn't cried sober since I was eleven. I looked at Gretchen. The five-foot shaft topped with the Spear of Destiny clutched in her fists, more like a warrior goddess worthy of all the world's riches. She had to know. She had to know all the things I'd thought but never said. She had to know all the things I'd said that came out wrong. She had to know all the dreams I had about her, for us.

Frank had his share of losing.

Almost Switch... Jammer... Faith in Humanity... Faith in Heaven...Fear of Hell...

And yet, as he admits in the song, Frank was amused by it all.

To be honest, I was struggling to find the humor.

Frank said screw being humble.

I smiled at Gretchen. She smiled back. Shy was never the style of either of us.

Ole Blue Eyes did it his way.

For good or ill, goddamned right we did.

Frank sang about the defining characteristics of a man, and what does a man possess.

Gretchen...

Frank sang about laying it all out on the table.

I looked to my left and saw Lucifer in all the glory of his Divine Birth, armored and decked out for war, a brace of three spears in his left hand and a spiked Morningstar in his right. He stood surrounded by his Infernal Host in their dread damnation.

I looked to my right and there stood Michael, probably Rafael and Gabrielle bedecked as you'd imagine warriors of the Throne; Michael with sword and shield, probably Rafael with a sword and ax, Gabrielle with a bow and arrows of light. The angelic armies arrayed in good order, prepared and ready for the Day that had come.

Like Rocky, Frank sang about taking the hits but moving through.

I looked at Gretchen. Our eyes touched for what might be the last time. She knew, she had to...

For the time had finally come upon us. Hell to the left, Heaven to the right. Gretchen and I in the center, standing at the End of All Things—upon the field of Armageddon.

Frank sang about doing it his way. *My Way* ended like the world was probably about to.

Goddamn, my girl has great taste in music

"Dying man couldn't make up his mind which place to go to – both have their advantages, Heaven for the climate, hell for the company!"

-Mark Twain's Notebooks and Journals, vol 3

Chapter One

Songs for the Non-Existent Foot Chase Mix
"Magnum PI Theme" Mike Post

E ver have one of those thoughts that are just completely random and inappropriate to the situation you might find yourself at that moment? Like *What's Kathy Ireland up to right now?* While you're sitting at a funeral? Or *What serial killer name would make the best name for a pet? Probably depends on the pet, right?* While you're sitting in a tax audit? Or the ever disturbing *I bet she's been fucking her work friend Glenn for years* while a should-be adorable four-year-old tells you a story about dreams of purple skies and rainbow milk.

In a totally inappropriate moment, I found myself wondering: *I wish someone would be nice to Adele. I mean listen to her music, even her upbeat songs are fucking sad if you pay attention to the lyrics. Shit, someone just give her a hug and say, "You're talented, sweet, lovely, and freaking valued."* And why would she want

Someone Like You? It obviously didn't work the first time, so why would you want to try the same thing again? Maybe Adele's crazy... All that running through my shallow kiddie pool of a brain as Gretchen and I tore down the sidewalk as fast as our feet would carry us.

Were this a movie, it would have all been in slow motion. Gretchen would definitely look better running in slow motion than me,. but to be fair, she looks better doing anything than I do. At that moment, her Doc Martens were basically soundless as she sprinted down the cracked sidewalk with a collapsed ASP club in each hand. Her raven hair was tied back in a ponytail and her bangs bounced with each step. She had a gray tanktop that read *Duct Tape, Mmmmm*. I don't know where she got it. Her pouch belt was wrapped around her slender waist above her short shorts that had at one point been acid-washed jeans. The rips in her fishnets were more alluring than they were a sign of our *not quite living in poverty but definitely not making it big* lifestyle.

In contrast to her full-speed gliding down the sidewalk, my black-and-white Chucks slapped the pavement with such a volume and form that any decent track coach or kinesiology professor would bust an aneurysm as opposed to finding the vocabulary to describe all the things I was doing wrong. I held my hands out straight like I was about to karate chop something and managed to pump my arms in relative time with my legs. I did manage to jump a stroller without knocking it or the baby in it over, all the while wondering, *What's up with Adele?'*

At that moment, I knew life would be better then if The Beastie Boy's *Sabotage* was blasting in the background, but life doesn't have a running soundtrack and I don't have a Foot Chase Mix. The simple reason being is I never really wanted to get in foot chases for the equally simple reasoning that foot chases are work...exhausting fucking work.

Normally P.I. work was just sitting around watching stuff and trying to not die of boredom while waiting to get pictures of people doing things they shouldn't be doing in the first place. Problem is, you gotta have clients. So when there was a lack of those annoying commodities, Gretchen cooked up a plan. We referred to it as 'The Plan' because we're not professional writers or acronym authors. It was simple; the cops are always putting out "reward for information leading to the arrest of" bullshit releases, so the first time Gretchen and I did their job for them, handed them their case, they stiffed us. "Sorry, your information wasn't pertinent to our arrest." It was bullshit, but not like we could really argue it.

So this time, we were going to catch the assholes, drag them to the station, hand them all the evidence we gathered and the assholes in question and then like pimps, get our fucking money.

That's why we found ourselves sprinting down the street at eleven twenty-three a.m., past the moms heading to the park to meet with their Mommy Groups, homeless people, and the occasional person who has a job just trying to get lunch from Larry Wilcox's hotdog cart, chasing Toshiro Some-Japanese-Surname-I-Can't-Fucking-Pronounce and the two guys who decided to run with him.

Toshiro went by the nickname—I refuse to say street name or street tag or whatever nomenclature dip shits are using nowadays— "Baby-Powder." He got the name because he likes selling to kids and getting kids to sell for him. He'd started selling dimebags in high school, coke in college, and now mainly sold designer shit like Molly but dabbled in a bit of everything. He dressed like an asshole who heard the term cyber-punk, but dressed as if they didn't look up what cyber-punk actually meant. He looked like a shithead in an Asian Sex Pistols cover band, but pushing forty as opposed to being an age appropriate for that kind of thing.

The two guys running with him were a little bit of an unknown. I was figuring the tall, bald, tubby one was his Mook Muscle, the skinny cracked-out looking bastard was either some kind of sycophant, or more likely a buyer, just caught up in shit that was falling on Toshiro.

I was really getting tired of running. I reached in and brushed the fire in my gut, the fire that was always there and felt the Wrath start flowing through me. I got faster, pulling ahead of Gretchen and starting to close on the trio of shitheads.

"Cheater!" Gretchen spat as I started pulling away. There was no venom to it and I could feel the laugh behind it.

The crack-skinny dude turned his head to glance behind him. He had a real pimple problem for a guy somewhere between the age of thirty and sixty. With his head facing the wrong way, he clipped a fire hydrant. The other two made no more to help that dude as he tumbled, in the words of Alanis Morrisette, *Head Over Feet*.

"I got him," I heard Gretchen call, so I passed the pile of crackhead without even pausing.

Coming up to the cross street I glanced and instantly leapt, doing my best Bo Duke across the hood of a screeching stopping car as opposed to the alternative of getting fucking creamed. No matter how cool a hood slide looks, it slows you down.

I pumped my legs and my light-gray suit jacket fanned out behind me, exposing my underarm pistol rig to anyone paying attention. The sprinting made it easy to keep the Wrath stoked.

I saw Baby-Powder look back and gasp to the surprisingly quick tubby bastard. "Get him!" Not the most thought-out or articulated plan I've ever heard but to his credit, that's what the mook tried to do. He turned and raised his fists in a manner that orated his intentions with aplomb.

What he didn't see coming was me just running around him, knowing he couldn't catch up without the previously established forward momentum. Plus, I knew Gretchen would be on him in a moment or two. She seemed to like going after big guys' knees.

As she'd told me more than once, "A knee's the great leveler."

I kept pumping my arms and legs and started to quickly gain ground on Toshiro. He kept glancing back and that kept costing him speed. I was only about twenty-five feet behind him when he turned into an alley. I was moving fast enough I half-jumped and planted a foot on the wall to angle myself into the alley.

About the time Toshiro got in the alley, he pulled out an honest-to-God butterfly knife and started flipping it open, then threw it at me.

The good news was two-fold. Buffed with the Wrath, I was fast enough to dodge it. On top of that, the dipshit did a bad job flipping it open and it had shut itself as it twirled through the air at me. So even if I hadn't gotten out of the way, worst I would have had to deal with would have been a bruise.

The ineptitude made me even more angry. I felt the Sword wanting to be unleashed.

I kept running at him and he raised his hands defensively. I have never understood why everyone expected me to fight via the Marquis of Queensbury rules.

With the Wrath buffing my strength, I kicked Toshiro Some-Japanese-Surname-I-Can't-Fucking-Pronounce right in his goddamned balls hard enough to lift both his feet off the ground. I stepped out of the way and watched as he fell to the ground, his body hitting perfectly flat.

"What the fuck were you thinking?" I half-laughed half-yelled at his prone form. He rolled onto his side and clutched at his crotch as he wept.

"I mean," I lectured as I paced slowly pack and forth before him as I tried to catch my breath. "I mean, I had to chase you three fucking blocks. What the shit, man? What was the plan?"

I bent down and started going through his pockets as he cried. I found a thick roll of twenties in one pocket and a short stack of hundreds in another. I figured that even if the cops stiffed us again this wasn't a total loss. I pocketed the dough. I also found bags of pills in the '90s-style fanny pack that ruined his wannabe Sex Pistols look. I left the pills there for the cops.

Slowly, he started getting his shit together enough to yell in an attempt to be intimidating. "Let go of me, you son of a bitch!"

I chuckled as I tried to count the money I was blatantly stealing. "Yeah, she was kind of a bitch."

Baby-Powder pushed himself up and started to try to run even as he was still bent in half. I grabbed him by the neck and pushed him head-first into the nearby dumpster. The impact sounded like the *clang* of the world's shittiest bell.

"Seriously, dude, what's the plan?" I repeated, still laughing. "Look, get up and stand with your hands on the wall. You've seen enough police procedural shows to know how this fucking works."

I watched him slowly get to his feet and lean with his hands against the wall. He was still crying, and I was as genuinely as sympathetic as the Death Valley is wet. I glanced back at the end of the alley, but Gretchen hadn't appeared yet. I knew three incontrovertible facts. Number one, Toshiro was an asshole. Number two, I could still feel the Wrath pulling at me. Number three, I wasn't a cop.

I kicked Baby-Powder in the crotch from behind and watched his knees buckle and give out from under him. After the second kick to the junk, I was positive that if Toshiro didn't already have kids, he wasn't having kids.

Score one for the gene pool's skim filter.

I grabbed him by the back of the neck and twisted an arm behind him, cranking it as I pulled him up and started walking him out of the alley. Near the end, I saw Gretchen standing with the other two on their knees before her, hands cuffed behind their backs.

She smiled sweetly then gestured at the closed butterfly knife on the ground. "What's up with that?"

I shrugged, then jerked Toshiro a little. "Fuck-nut here threw a closed butterfly knife at me."

She put her hand over her mouth but couldn't stifle the giggle. "Surly you can't be serious?"

I smirked. She'd set it up on purpose so I couldn't deny letting her have it. "I'm very serious, and don't call me 'Shirley.'"

She gestured with a phone she must have gotten off the crackhead or the mook. "I got us an Uber, four-and-a-half minutes out—on these guys." Her smile was infectious.

"You guys are the best, you know that?" I pushed Toshiro down to his knees as we waited.

Not a bad day at all, all things considered anyway. Despite all the running.

Chapter Two

No Way Of Knowing
"Hell on High Heels" Motley Crüe

I would be willing to bet that angels possess a different sense of time than us little folk. Maybe that's why it took Gabrielle almost six months to knock on the office door after Gretchen and I retrieved the Spear of Destiny.

It was a Sunday morning; Agnes didn't come in on Sundays. I heard the rapping on the door to the office and my eyes opened with the speed of a sloth that had eaten a whole tray of pot brownies. I felt the warmth of Gretchen's body pressed against me and the familiar dull ache that accompanies a man when he wakes in the morning with a statue-worthy beauty held tight in his arms and the firmness of her form pressing to the relative firmness of his. I could smell the hint of lavender shampoo as my face was buried in it. My right arm was under her head under the pillow with my 1911 grasped in my hand. My left arm was draped over her naked hips.

I shifted slightly and felt the brushing of metal as the slide of my 1911 brushed the barrel of her custom single-action Army Colts. As much as I didn't want to, I extricated myself from the responsibility of the big spoon. I don't think I woke her, but if I did she was either good-natured enough to let me think I hadn't or she simply drifted back into the sweet oblivion of slumber.

I pulled on the slacks I had worn the day before and the two days preceding those. I pulled a T-shirt over my head and tucked the pistol in the back of my waist as I stealthed my way out of the side room of the office suite. I shut the door behind me and could see the outline of someone through the powdered-and-painted glass of the office door. I passed Agnes's immaculately organized desk. In her outbox was the bill for the Crossfield jobs. Mr. and Mrs. both hired us to dig up dirt on the other. I'm guessing there should have been ethical concerns that should have precluded us from taking one or the other, but we took them anyway. We got pictures of Mr. Crossfield with Mrs. Crossfield's sister the same evening we got pictures of Mrs. Crossfield playing an interesting game of Twister with the best man from their wedding twenty years ago. Their college-aged daughter and high school senior son probably weren't going to be overly pleased with how things of their seemingly normal family had turned out in reality to be.

Reality can be a great disappointment in the end.

Besides that in Agnes's inbox was the check for Melvin Ludlow job. Gretchen and I, with the help of The Grand Vizier Megatron Terabyte the Cyber Samurai, had managed to track down an identity thief. Turns out it was Mr. Ludlow's homeowners association president. He'd done the dirty with the identity of several other members of the condo complex that Ludlow lived in, but they hadn't paid us so we didn't feel a need to tell them.

As was, when those checks got cashed, we could afford to keep the doors open, and Agnes paid for the next three months baring some insane expensive circumstance. Life seemed all right.

And then I opened the door.

"Goddamnit," I muttered as I saw her standing calmly. She seemed to have weathered the wait it took for me to get up and to the door with a dignity that shined a deceptively demure passivity.

She pouted. "Watch the blasphemy, please." The Southern twang to her voice seemed out of place considering where she was from.

"Gabrielle." I sighed and stood aside so she could step in. "Shouldn't the Herald of fucking Heaven be at church or something?" I looked at my wrist and remembered I didn't wear a watch anyway.

She laughed with a good nature. "That's cute, Nick." She reached into her purse and pulled out a white envelope, the type you'd put an eight-by-ten photograph in. It was crisp-edged and not bent even though it shouldn't have fit like that in the purse. It was sealed with a blue wax that matched her eyes. The bottom of the envelope bulged. "Your payment for services rendered, my good sir."

The seal in the wax was a trumpet, but not stylized; it was a Louis Armstrong-looking trumpet. I broke it and opened the edge, peering in. Inside were five car titles and five sets of keys.

I shut the top and tossed the envelope to my desk. One of the envelope's crisp corners crinkled like a fender in an accident as it hit the desk and fell to the floor with a rattle of keys. I ignored it.

"Thanks," I said even as a yawn slurred my speech. I gestured to the door. "Nice of you to drop by."

She smiled, but it held disappointment. "No, now, Nick, I've held up my end. Now it's your turn."

"And what's that?" I just wanted to crawl back in bed.

"The Spear." She smiled demurely. "The deal was for the Spear."

I shook my head. "No, it wasn't."

"Oh?" She kept smiling but now it felt predatory.

"The deal was we make sure the Satanist didn't give the Spear to a demon. That didn't happen, so our deal is done." I gestured to the door. "Thanks for dropping by."

"Nick," she said with an acute stroke of politic deftness. "There was an understood implication—"

"If wishes were kisses," I interrupted her and didn't care, "then I wouldn't have been a fuckless virgin for as long as I was."

"Nick..." Her patience was annoying this early in the morning.

"I'm open for a new deal but as it stands we're keeping the Spear." I walked over to the desk and opened my drawer. All that sat inside was Jammer's nickel-plated Kimber 1911, a glass, and a mostly empty bottle of Macallan 18. I left the glass there and picked up the bottle.

"Fine, what do you suggest?" she asked with a smile that was slightly deflated by the narrowing of her eyes.

I met her gaze and didn't break it. It felt like a chicken race and I wasn't swerving first. I tug/twisted the cork from the end of the bottle and took a long slow tug from the neck. Letting the hair of the dog play over my tongue before swallowing. "I want Jammer back."

There, sadly, was no hesitation. "That's not in the cards, Nick. That can't even be put on the table."

I pushed the cork back into the bottle and replaced it in the drawer. "Then we're done here." Once again I gestured to the door. "So unless you got any other business...?"

"What about Baalberieth?" she asked with her hand on her hip, giving her a sassier look than you'd expect an Angel to have.

Again we played the ocular chicken race. "Why is that my problem?"

"Is that how you want to play this?" Her voice was sweet, but lemonade tastes best cold.

"I think you waited six months form the last job to come pay me so either you're a bad customer, or you were waiting for something else." I pointed to the door. "So fucking spill it or let me get back to bed."

"Baalberieth hasn't killed anyone since he was summoned to this world, Nick." She spoke like a teacher, but I wasn't getting the lesson.

"I'm leaning back on why this is my goddamned problem." I wanted to reach for the bottle again but I didn't.

"Baalberieth is the Demon of Murder, but he's more. He's also the Secretary and Witness of Hell." Again, she was talking but it wasn't sinking in.

"So, Hell lost its notary. What's the fucking problem?" I felt my fingers go to the drawer but instead, I rested my hand on the top of the desk.

"Were he here killing we could deal with this ourselves, but he's not. We need to know what he's up to." She crossed her arms before her and leaned back against Agnes's desk.

"Define *we*." My eyes were narrowed; it's easy to be suspicious of someone who takes six months to pay you for a job that cost you.

"The Throne." She said the name like that explained everything.

"What's the scratch?" I wished Agnes were here to take notes.

"What do you want?" That question actually sounded honest.

"Jammer."

She looked genuinely regretful as she shook her head. "I'm sorry, Nick, but that's never going to be on the table."

I chewed my lip for a moment. "Can you get Switch back to a hundred percent?"

She met my eyes. I don't know what she was expecting me to ask for but it wasn't that. It's odd the look in an angel's eyes when they were surprised. "Yes, I can."

"Okay." I nodded. I held my hand out to shake.

She walked out to me and reached in, her hand was small in mine, and my hands aren't big. Her skin was soft and cool but her grip was firm as our hands went up and down twice.

She turned and finally started to the door.

"How do I reach you?" I asked as I yawned.

"Don't you know?" she asked mischievously as she looked back over her shoulder.

"What?" I asked. "I suppose to pray or something?"

She laughed. "You really think anyone is paying attention to your never-sent prayers, Nick Decker?"

I said *fuck it* and pulled the bottle back out and worked the cork. "No, I guess not."

She smiled. "I'll email Agnes my contact details."

"Probably better than telling me," I agreed.

She stopped at the door and turned to face me. "There is a clock on this, Nick."

I didn't say anything. She could tell me or she wouldn't but I wasn't going to ask. It was a combination of too much pride and too damned tired to ask. I did take another drink.

"You have a week, Nick."

I nodded; one way or another I'd get it done for Switch.

She stepped into the hall and was gone. There was no shadow against the door, no sound of heels in the hallway. She was just gone.

I put the bottle back and pulled my 1911 out from the back of my pants. I walked slowly back into the bedroom/kitchen/living room combo. I hit the can before coming back to the bed stripping back down to the nothing I was accustomed to sleeping in.

The bed was new, a double. I'd found the mattress and box springs still wrapped up in plastic when I'd broken into Jammer's place to clean it up so no one would find anything they shouldn't. I took what medical supplies I knew what to do with, a handful of guns, a few T-shirts that were his favorites. I got rid of the drugs, mainly weed and mescaline, and took the sex toys off the window sills. I'd had to break in through the window, but once I got the doors open I'd let Joy with an E-Y come in. She'd cried but taken nothing.

But now Gretchen and I had a bed where the pull-out couch used to be. We had to push it half into the kitchen area to get in the closet or push it in front of the closet to get it out of the kitchen area, but it was an honest-to-God bed that didn't leave us lying on a pull-out with a metal goddamned bar under our asses.

I slid back into the bed, my gun arm back under the pillow, our bodies lining up in our spooning. I smelled the lavender in her hair and felt her warmth. Her touch felt like good whiskey tasted. I closed my eyes and drifted back to sleep content with her in my arms.

I had no idea of the storm that was approaching. I had no idea the trouble Gabrielle had just gotten us into. I had no way of knowing it was the last good sleep I'd have before Armageddon.

Chapter Three

The Best Part of Waking Up
"I Got You Babe" Sonny and Cher... think Groundhog Day

People have told me I'm a pain in the ass in the morning, but I'm nothing compared to Gretchen. Some people have pep and get up and go; I might be bad, but she's worse. The coffee pot sitting in the kitchen was for her. I'd never been a coffee drinker. I'd seen too many people who were useless until they had their first cup of coffee and I'd decided I'd rather be useless all fucking day. That said, even though I didn't drink coffee didn't mean I didn't appreciate waking up to the smell.

I opened my eyes to the sight of Gretchen standing in a pair of black boy-cut panties with her back to me. I let my eyes glide over her tattooed wings as she stood topless with her back to me, her raven hair falling over her shoulders.

"You awake yet?" she asked.

I smiled and rolled from my side onto my back. "How did you know?"

She laughed and flipped her hair over one shoulder as she looked back to me over her other shoulder. "I didn't, that was the third time I asked."

That got a laugh out of me, too. "Fair fuckin' enough."

"So what's the plan on our off day?" she asked as I heard her pour the black life-imbuing liquid into her mug.

"We got a job." I thought back over the conversation with Gabrielle.

"Who's?" She sipped the same way kids slurp soup.

"Gabrielle." I looked, but from the back I couldn't really tell her reaction.

"She pay for the last one?" Gretchen looked back to me before topping off the mug.

I nodded.

"What's the stakes of this one?" I liked how she didn't ask about the job, just the payment. My short stripper was as mercenary as I was, I guess. Soulmates.

I chewed my lip, unsure of if I should tell her. "Well..."

She turned and crossed one arm under her perky tits and the other lifted the mug. "Well?"

I made sure to look into Gretchen's eyes. "She's gonna fix Switch."

Gretchen smiled and nodded. "And Jammer?"

I shook my head and her nod stopped but the smile stayed. "Well, we got to do it for Switch."

I nodded. "Yeah, that was my thought."

"We shouldn't tell him, though," she added before drinking more of her morning joe.

I didn't say anything; I simply raised my eyebrows.

"We shouldn't get his hopes up," she explained. "Especially because I'm guessing whatever it is she wants is liable to get us killed. Cause I'm doubting she's going to pay in that case."

I nodded.

"So what's the job?" Gretchen smiled, the coffee having an effect in reviving her optimistic demeanor.

"We need to figure out what Baalberieth is up to," I said and let it hang there.

Gretchen laughed. "Oh, that's all?"

I shrugged; that got another laugh from her.

"So where do we start?" she asked as I turned my back to her and kicked my legs out of the bed. I stood, arched my back, and popped my knuckles. I was getting older. Indiana Jones had said, "It's not the years, it's the mileage." That bastard knew what the hell he was talking about.

I dug my knuckles into my lower back and walked around the bed. "A shower. I'm starting with a shower."

She laughed as I shambled into the bathroom. I got the hot water going and stepped behind the yellow rubber ducky shower curtain.

I felt the hot water flow over my head, matting my short unruly hair to my scalp as I leaned my head forward and let the water and steam flow. It wasn't long until I felt the curtain open and close before feeling her arms slide around me and her wet body pressing up behind me. "It's not your fault, Nick," she whispered.

"I know," I muttered as water streamed down my face, "and I don't."

"I know," she said and kissed my back.

I lifted my head and opened my mouth, getting a mouthful of water. I sloshed it and gargled before spitting directly at the drain.

I felt her take the bar of soap and start scrubbing my back. I waited till I felt her reach around and start scrubbing my crotch with the bar and I laughed. She handed me the bar. I scrubbed my hair into a good lather and washed my face. I rinsed it off before I scrubbed my shoulders and chest. I washed down and got my legs and feet. Gretchen helped steady me as I washed my feet and rinsed them.

I turned around and faced her. "Washing you is more fun."

She laughed and I set my bar of soap down and grabbed hers. My soap felt rougher than hers. I stepped out of the way of the water and let her rinse down as I started scrubbing her shoulders and back.

"So what's the play?" she asked.

"Well, I'm gonna reach around and cop a feel in a minute," I confessed.

She laughed and looked back playfully, but she didn't stop me.

"So?" she asked.

"Your tits or the plan?" I asked as I used the soap as an excuse to enjoy myself.

"Both?" She laughed.

"Phenomenal and as shitty as they usually are," I confessed.

"Which is which?" I could hear the smile in her voice even as she faced away from me.

"I'd take your tits over one of my plans any day." I was rewarded as she pressed her ass back.

She wiggled her hips. "You know, you tell me the plan and we can take care of that." She pushed back for emphasis.

"We'll start with Megatron digging on the Akashic Network, see what that rattles out of the trees." She laughed at how quick I answered.

We made love in the shower and then washed up again before the water got too cold. I pulled on a charcoal Armani suit Uncle Lew gave me and a plain white shirt; never a tie. I was tugging on my black-and-white Chucks as Gretchen got dressed in tight yoga pants, her pouch belt, a black Sharky's tank top, and her leather half-jacket. I slid on my underarm rig, my OD Green Springfield 1911 under my left arm, and then I went to the drawer to slide Jammer's nickel-plated Kimber under my right arm. I slid my flask in my right inside pocket and my wallet of fake credentials in the left. On my belt, I had four spare 1911 magazines. I slid my phone in the pocket with the wallet as less temptation to get the flask. I went ahead and pulled on my pair of Wayfarers.

I tossed the camera to Gretchen because honestly, she was a way better shutterbug than I would ever be. Her photo composition made shots of affairs almost seem like art. Not that anyone would accuse me of understanding art. Oddly, her photography had gotten a lot better since the events with her Mom.

She dried and combed her hair as I brushed my teeth then I got the fuck out of her way in terms of ownership of the bathroom.

I left a note for Agnes in case we didn't make it back before the world's greatest assistant arrived for work on Monday.

Gretchen took a styrofoam cup and filled it with the rest of the coffee. I respected that she took it black. In a way, it was as indicative as how low maintenance she was. In fact, even though Bruce Campbell had warned me I could screw up with my soulmate, it was really Gretchen's accommodating nature that made us work.

Who else would put up with me?

We headed out and took the stairs instead of the suspect elevator. Megatron had moved into one of the empty offices on my floor, but we weren't going there yet. Job or no, Sunday was for brunch with Yuri and Mary Jo. Mary Jo understood my proclivity for "non-fancy" food so she chose the brunch places with me in mind.

Gretchen's styrofoam cup of coffee was only enough to get her to her next cup of coffee. The restaurant was five blocks away so we walked.

"What's this place called?" I asked.

Gretchen sipped her coffee and looked at her phone. "The Red Door Knob."

"Fuck."

She laughed at that reaction but I dunno what else she could have expected from me.

"This place Old Person Eclectic or Hipster Bullshit?"

She laughed again. "I dunno, didn't ask."

"Goddamnit," I muttered as we stopped for a bus to drive by.

"You look hungover." She smiled up at me as she clutched my arm.

"I'm not as young as I used to be. Can't drink like I'm twenty-five anymore." They say confession is good for the soul but that's bullshit. Or at least that's how it felt then.

Her laugh didn't help things.

Where my eating could be defined as picky, Yuri was a goddamned garbage disposal. His idea of edible was synonymous with *able to chew without breaking teeth for the most part.* Mary Jo seemed to be a fan of fancy for fancy's sake in terms of brunch. The first we'd attended I couldn't even tell you what was on the menu; I didn't even recognize the language. I didn't have a lot of hope for The Red Door Knob.

I didn't get hopeful when I saw the place. It looked like it was designed to resemble some cafe in France where Hemingway would have written the more depressing bits of *The Sun Also Rises*. The owners wanted it to feel so Parisian that no French person would ever be caught dead there. Luckily the weather was warm enough that Yuri and Mary Jo had taken a table outside. That would make it easier to throw myself in front of a bus if the waiter offered me kale-infused water or *quinoa* anything.

Mary Jo hugged me low enough around the waist she pointedly didn't know if I had pistols under my arms. Yuri lifted Gretchen off the ground as he hugged her.

We sat, Yuri and I with our backs against the wall and the girls across from us. I picked up the hard-cover menu and saw it had easily eight pages consisting of a card stock that had a higher thread count than my towel.

Mary Jo laughed. "Page three, Nick, halfway down."

I looked skeptically and then my eyes went wide. "Holy shit." I didn't believe it so I read it again. *Savory smoked bacon waffle with honey cinnamon butter and hot syrup.* My eyes were wide as I looked at Mary Jo.

"Oh, ye of little faith." She laughed.

I shut the menu, I didn't need to look at it anymore. "Hey, even fucking Thomas wanted to poke his fingers in Christ's holes, all right?"

She laughed again. "Okay, forgiven."

I didn't wait a lot of time when the waiter arrived. Gretchen ordered eggs Benedict, a coffee, and a mimosa; Mary Jo ordered something I couldn't pronounce and a Bloody Mary. Yuri ordered about three things off the menu; none of them I think were in English.

I think the reasoning behind Sunday brunch was for Mary Jo to keep an eye on me and Gretchen. I think she worried about us. The mothering was a touch odd for us; neither of us had possessed award-winning moms. But in a way it was sweet. Their kids were gone in college and I was willing to bet that we were the target of empty nest syndrome. I'd always thought of Yuri as a cool uncle and Mary Jo as an overly protective aunt. But I was as shitty an uncle as I had been a son, so how would I know?

I think after Jammer died Mary Jo was afraid I would flounder. I hoped that was the reasoning. Truth is I think Yuri felt guilty we'd left him out of the play that had cost us Jammer.

What if are the two shittiest words in the English language.

Gretchen smiled throughout, and no coffee could ever compare to that.

Chapter Four

Beating the Bushes
"Lookin for Love in all the Wrong Places" - Covered by Me First
and the Gimmie Gimmie's

W e went back to the building and made our way to our floor. The offices of the office B-4 was no longer occupied by Cleveland Guthrie CPA. Cleveland had bolted from the country one night without a word to friends or family. As far as we knew he was holed up on some non-extradition beach living off a lot of other people's money. I'd lucked out in that all he did was my taxes; he didn't manage anything for me. Not that I really had much money to manage.

Now the office space B-4 was occupied by *Megan T. Meyer Cyber Solutions*. She was basically doing the same work she was doing before. Cybersecurity consulting and network planning and whatever other buzzword phrases could be thrown at computers and the things people did with them nowadays.

I rapped my knuckles on her powdered glass window and waited for her to come to the door. To my great disappointment, she answered the door in her idiotic geisha outfit, complete with cheap Chinese-made sword.

I sighed. "Goddamnit…"

"What?" Megatron asked with genuine confusion.

"Why?" I shook my head.

"Why what?" Her confusion had not abated.

I gestured at the outfit. "Why are you the way you fucking are?"

"Oh my god," I heard Gretchen gasp. "I LOVE IT!" She rushed past me and wrapped Megatron up in a tight hug. The other side effect of Jammer's death was Joy with an E-Y didn't talk to us anymore. Apparently, it was just too hard for her. Gretchen had fought it, hard, but one person can't hang on when the other is hell-bent on letting go. Jammer's death had cost Gretchen both her mother and Joy. So the void of best girlfriend was filled by Megatron. It didn't help that she was living in the same hall as us either. Proximity matters in relationships as much as it matters in non-gerrymandered census taking. So when Gretchen had told Megatron when they first met, "We are going to be the best of friends!" it turned out to be prophetic.

Gretchen's hug elicited a squeal from Megatron and a wish to commit suicide from me.

"How was brunch?" Megatron asked with a giggle.

"Oh, it was amazing. Mary Jo found a place that Nick even liked!" Gretchen laughed.

Even though Megatron's look resembled mock disbelief, I knew it was genuine. "Nick doesn't like anything."

"I know!" Gretchen giggled. She looked up and down Megatron's outfit. "I want this kimono." I tried to imagine Gretchen in the kimono but I couldn't separate just the kimono out of the outfit. I pictured Gretchen in the whole Megatron insanity. Somehow Gretchen made it appealing.

"It was handcrafted in Singapore," Megatron bragged.

"So you're saying it's not Japanese?" I asked. My curiosity got me dirty looks from both ladies. "What?" Instead of addressing my question, the ladies chose to ignore me.

"Mega," Gretchen smiled, "we need a favor."

"Sure, Gretchen, what do you need?" Megatron was always helpful when Gretchen did the asking. It was like pulling freaking teeth when I needed anything.

"We need," Gretchen said cautiously, "you to do some tugging on the Akashic Network."

Megatron's eyes narrowed into the suspicious glare that she normally saved for me and graciously let Gretchen experience it. "You remember what happened last time I started tugging on that web?"

Gretchen took both of Megatron's hands in hers. "It's important. It could help Switch."

It was honest, but that didn't make it less of a low blow. It's a card I'd have played, but I wasn't sure Gretchen would have. But she did. Then again that's all it took.

Megatron stepped aside and let us in, shutting the door behind us. Whereas Gretchen and mine's office could have been ripped from the set of *The Maltese Falcon*, with the exception of Agnes's laptop anyway, Megatron's was like something out of *The Matrix*. Two walls filled with various monitors displaying everything from reruns of *Naruto* to current stock trends for various global markets. Her leather swivel chair had controls for something on the arms, but for all I knew they might as well have controlled a spaceship.

"Okay, for Switch," Mega agreed. Yet instead of walking over to one of the various touchscreens or keyboards, she walked to a file cabinet. "What do you need to find?"

"Baalberieth," I told her flatly, I didn't see a reason to sugar coat anything. Then again that could probably be a big problem with my general life philosophy.

She pulled open a drawer and started pulling on a pair of gloves with wires running up the backs of each of her fingers and LED lights that I was positive were just there to look freaking weird. She then pulled out a VR headset that probably came in four sizes: small, normal, abnormal, and asshole. It doesn't take a genius to guess which size Megatron Terabyte the Cyber Samurai chose to buy. She tugged her hair back and put the set on her hair, adjusting the head strap before connecting the chin strap. The straps were black and I could just imagine the chin strap coming away caked in white wannabe geisha makeup.

She started waving her hands around like a professional community theater actress trying to preform a farcical pantomime of Tom Cruise's performance in *Minority Report*. I wanted to scream but I managed to keep my trap shut and not make any grunting or growling animal sounds. It was the acting performance of a career. And the Oscar goes to….

"Okay," Megatron said as dramatically as anyone can say *okay,* "what do you need to know?"

"Can you print us off a general rundown, and then anything current?" Maybe it was the asshole in me or the Wrath of God I was carrying around in my gut, but I wanted to smash that VR set and tie her to her crazy chair instead of watching her wave her arms like a high school drama club understudy.

But I kept my shit together, and she kept waving her arms. "Oh," she whispered, and wiggled her fingers like she was doing jazz hands. "Oh!"

"Are you looking at VR-POV porn?" Gretchen asked in the most polite tone I could imagine.

"Should we leave?" I butted in, not wanting to know if the answer was yes.

"Nick, Gretchen, this…this is bad."

"Well," I said more calmly than I felt, "it's the fucking Demon of Murder."

"No, Nick." She flicked a wrist and pics started flashing on one of the monitors. "Dr. Eric Travis…he's still teaching."

"Doc Douchebag is dead." I was speaking slowly but watching the monitor. I knew it because I was there when he gave himself to the fucking demon.

She flicked her wrist again and an online announcement appeared on the screen. It was an advertisement for a lecture on *Feminine Symbolism in Egyptian Iconography: Comparing and Contrasting Within The Modern Paradigm*.

I looked at the announcement and at the picture of the smiling, Rolf wannabe from *The Sound of Music* in a three-piece suit standing behind a lectern, hand raised pointing at something off-screen.

"You're telling me for the past six months, the Demon of Murder has been posing as a douchebag college professor?" I wasn't asking anyone in particular, I just kinda felt like it needed to be said.

"Well," Gretchen offered, "this isn't so bad."

"How is this not bad?" Megatron asked as she twirled her gloved fingers, probably scrolling through something. Hopefully scrolling through something, any other possibility I could think of was too horrible to contemplate.

"Well," Gretchen chewed her lower lip while looking for a bright side. "We know where he lives, where he works, where he'll be the day after tomorrow." She gestured to the notice still on the screen.

"I don't know if it helps," Megatron said, unable to hide the concern in her voice. "I think someone else is looking for him, too."

"Well, that's good too, right?" Gretchen grinned. "Enemy of my enemy?"

"Who else is looking for this asshole, Mega?" I asked quietly. My focus was still on Baalberieth. The picture of Dr. Douchebag up on the monitor.

"Uriel."

"What the fuck kind of parent names a kid Uriel?" I asked offhandedly, derisively. "Shit head have a surname?"

I glanced at Gretchen and saw genuine concern on her face.

"Nick," Mega said slowly, "Uriel is an archangel."

That set on me a bit heavy. I'd dealt with three archangels so far in my life. Gabby, who brought us work that so far, the one job really, was more trouble than it'd been worth. Michael, who had shown up at Jammer's wake. Michael had been cordial, but in the way that opponents could be courteous before a fight—the politeness of *I respect you but am going to fuck you the fuck up* courtesy. Then lastly there was Zadkiel. That had ended better than expected. I'd cut Zadkiel's fucking head off.

"Can you see why Uriel's in town?" I silently hoped it was for some unrelated innocuous reason. Deep down I knew I wasn't lucky enough for the reasoning to be *He's here for a bake sale!*

"I can't see anything obvious," Megatron confessed.

"Why would Heaven double book this?" Gretchen asked.

"What do you mean?" I glanced at her and saw her concern as she chewed her lip nervously.

"Why would Gabrielle put us on this job," Gretchen gestured to the picture of Dr. Douchebag on the screen, "if Uriel was already on this?"

"It could be messed up corporate structure," Megatron offered.

"Huh?" Gretchen's confusion was apparent in her Shakespearean repose.

"Well," Megatron offered as we heard her industrial-strength printer start to spit paper, "you know a corperation, or really any big organization. All the parts don't necessarily talk to each other. I mean, did Gabrielle put you on this job or did someone put her to put you on this job? I mean, we don't know if they work dependent or independent of each other."

We mulled that in the relative quiet except for the printer noises and computer fans.

"Michael didn't go after you at Jammer's wake but I'm pretty sure Zadkiel would have." Gretchen nodded in agreement to an argument Megatron hadn't really made, but the supposition was there.

"Gabrielle doesn't want the Sword," I agreed, "so you're saying the Heavenly Choirs aren't on the same sheet of music?"

"Well, that makes sense with what Lucifer told us about why Zadkiel was coming after the Sword." Gretchen was starting to sound more excited than she should have been with this kind of thing.

"Yeah, but even without a band leader, these assholes have to talk to each other, right?" I mean, come on, Heaven couldn't be as fucked up as the corporate world where asshats didn't talk to each other except at meetings. How often would heaven have meetings? What's time matter to immortals?

Then it dawned on me what I needed to do, even if I didn't want to, really didn't want to. "Fuck."

Megatron started pulling off her idiotic VR rig and Gretchen looked to me in confusion. "What?" Gretchen asked as her fingers played up the inside of my arm.

"I gotta go to storage," I said quietly. "I gotta go through the box of stuff we took from Jammer's."

Megatron put her VR rig away and looked to Gretchen and me with concern. Last time something like this had happened she'd almost been taken and killed, Switch had been fucked up, and Jammer killed. Her concern was justified.

"What do we need from the Jammer box?" Gretchen asked. After Jammer had died we'd gone through his loft and cleaned it up, taken things no one needed to find. There'd been some guns, some medical stuff, and a lot of drugs we'd tossed.

I looked and let my gaze lock with Gretchen's dark, concerned eyes. "I need the mescaline." Her eyes went as wide as they were infinitely deep. "I need to talk to Bruce Campbell."

Chapter Five

...Still Drinking Fireball
"The Gambler" Kenny Rogers

S o, despite the fact that I come across as a scumbag, and the fact that I drink like a fish, I've never really done drugs. I mean I can't say I've never done drugs because back in the Army I was basically hooked on eight hundred milligrams of ibuprofen to the point that, like everyone else, I referred to them as "Ranger Candy." I've also taken whatever was prescribed to me because I've been sick. So when I say I've never really done drugs just take it to mean I've never done illegal shit or abused the stuff I was prescribed—except for the ibuprofen. I've used the hell out of that.

The only exceptions were the contact highs I've gotten at concerts, and the time Jammer dosed me with mescaline after I'd been shot in the shoulder. I never smoked coke, I've never snorted a line of weed—did I mix those up? To me, Molly is a girl's name and ecstasy is something found right at the end of sex. So the fact that Gretchen and I were lying side by side on the bed, fully clothed, holding hands, in the middle of the day was noteworthy because of the empty vials of concentrated mescaline laying in the garbage can, courtesy of Jammer.

I was pretty sure I'd not fallen asleep because I was just lying there staring at the stained tiles in the ceiling. So if I were asleep that definitely rated as the shittiest dream ever. Also, 1994 Kathy Ireland hadn't shown up yet, further evidence I wasn't dreaming. I lie waiting, gently moving my thumb and rubbing the soft skin between Gretchen's thumb and forefinger. It gave me something to focus on, and it felt nice.

We'd both agreed beforehand to not look at each other, because that might evolve into kissing, touching, doing it, and that would be a horrible state for your shared guardian angel to catch you.

I glanced down past my feet as I heard the knock on the door from the office. "You two decent?"

I smiled as I heard the rich voice call through the door. "Yeah." I squeezed Gretchen's hand and sat up in the bed, kicking my legs over the side and moving to the door, opening it.

There he stood, in a finely tailored black suit that made me think of when Sam Axe would play his alias Chuck Finley on *Burn Notice*. Bruce Campbell raised the bottle of Fireball whiskey to his lips and took a good tug. "You know, I shouldn't encourage the drug use."

"Sorry." I scratched the top of my head. "I didn't know how else to vision quest and we needed to talk."

"I don't know about WE needing to talk." He smiled. "But I do agree that YOU needed to talk."

"Yeah," I agreed. "Thus the mescaline."

He smiled and shook his head with genuine disapproval.

"What?" I asked a little offended at his juxtaposition. "Not like you left me a goddamned cellphone number or anything."

He *tsked* and took another sip of Fireball. "Come on, Nick, watch the blasphemy."

I felt Gretchen slide in next to me under my arm. I reflexively gave her a squeeze which, gratifyingly, she leaned into.

Bruce smiled and held out his hand to Gretchen. "I'm your guardian angel by the way."

Gretchen smiled as she shook his hand. "I'm a huge fan, and Nick told me. It's an honor."

He sighed. "You know, I'm not really Bruce Campbell, right?"

Gretchen giggled. "Yeah, but you'll do."

That made me laugh.

"So," Bruce said, obviously trying to change the subject, "what do you need to talk about?"

"Baalberieth."

He smiled and shook his head. "Can't help you there, kid, different team."

That was a little deflating. "Uriel?"

His eyebrows shot up at that one. "What about Uriel?"

"Why is he in town?" Gretchen asked as she reached out, letting her fingers brush over his forearm. It was like she wanted to see if he was real but didn't want to be obvious or impolite about it.

"She." Bruce smiled glancing down at Gretchen's hand, having obviously figured out what she was doing.

"She?"

He nodded. "Uriel's female, or at least form's female; it's not like angels are really anything. Archangels more so." He turned and sauntered back into the office and Gretchen and I followed. We oddly, naturally took our places behind our desks and Bruce settled himself into one of the chairs. "So, what do you want to know about Uriel?"

"What's he like?" Gretchen asked as she kicked her feet up on the corner of the desk.

"She," he corrected. "Well, all the archangels had a purpose. Zadkiel the Bannerman, Gabrielle the Herald, Michael the Champion, blah blah blah. Get it? Well, Uriel was the Watcher."

I felt my brow furrow and for a moment was surprised I didn't have wrinkles between my eyes to match my crow's feet. "Was?"

Bruce shrugged and lifted the bottle of Fireball back to his lips. "Well, everything got cocked up when your uncle Lucifer blew the coop, didn't it?"

"How so?"

Bruce leaned forward to set the bottle on the desk. "Well, he was supposed to be the big Who-Ha. He was supposed to manage the house while the Father got busy doing Father stuff. But without Lucifer behind the wheel, the car went a little nuts. It really didn't bother us lesser choirs, didn't really mess with my job at all. But the archangels..." He shrugged and held his hands out helplessly. "They're stuck doing jobs that were never really theirs to deal with."

"Such as?" Gretchen asked, while switching which foot was on top of the other.

I saw Bruce check out her shapely calf and as much thigh as he could gander. I figured that was an affectation he took on with the persona he'd chosen for Gretchen and me, and not really our guardian angel checking out my soulmate. But who the hell knows?

"Well, Michael was just supposed to be the Champion, but now he's running the War Host of Heaven, because who else could do it? Gabrielle was just supposed to be the Herald, but as you've figured out, she's also the—how would you call it?—the Pelopetentary of the Throne?"

"The fuck does that mean?" I blurted.

Bruce smiled like he'd forgotten for a moment what level of dumbass I was. "Super ambassador with deal-making powers."

"Okay."

"So, Uriel, her job changed. She was the Chief Watcher and responsible for stuff like the sun." He chuckled. "There's a human apocryphal story about Lucifer finding earth because of Uriel, but that's just silly. For as disorganized as things around the Throne can be now, part of the reason is Lucifer was really good at his job and he left a vacuum behind him."

"So, Uriel?" I was trying to put the train back on the tracks even as it seemed to be running full-steam ahead.

"So, Uriel," he smiled and clapped his hands to his knees, "went from Chief Watcher to the Huntress of Heaven."

"Well, that's a fucking leap, isn't it?" I groaned; shit wasn't getting any better. Why could no one ever give us good news?

He raised an eyebrow and cocked his famous chin out as he looked up, mock thoughtfully. "Is it? What do hunters do but watch and wait? Isn't that the majority of the job? The killing is really the smallest bit, right? So who would be better at hunting than the Throne's perfect watcher, who is immortal, so waiting isn't a concern?"

Gretchen nodded, showing she had no issue with following the logic Bruce was laying out for us. "So what's she hunting?"

Bruce leaned his elbows on his knees and smiled. "I have no idea."

"What do you mean you don't know?" You could hear the crushing frustration in Gretchen's voice. Like hope was standing on a rug and Bruce just jerked it out from under.

Bruce laughed. He held his hand up above his head. "Okay, you're talking about archangels, they're up here." He wiggled his hand a little. Then he dropped his hand down to just above the armrest of his chair. "I'm just guardian angel, I'm right here. So do you think folks up here," he shot his hand back over his head, "talk to folks down here?" He brought his hand back down.

Gretchen chewed her lip. The silence hung in the air and Bruce sat with a quizzical look on his face. The silence was heavy like a straight jacket. "No?" Gretchen finally offered.

Bruce golf clapped. "Plus," he added, "even if I did know, which I don't, I doubt I'd be able to tell you."

"Fair enough." I nodded. I was in the Army long enough to get how classified and privileged information worked.

"Thanks for understanding." I watched Bruce Campbell pick the bottle of Fireball up.

I reached in my drawer and pulled out my Macallan bottle. Gretchen grabbed glasses, and I poured two then looked to Bruce. "Want one?"

He smiled and shook the Fireball bottle. "Thanks, but I'm good. Your good stuff would be wasted on me."

"What do you know about Baalberieth?" I asked as I put the bottle up.

"Not much more than you." Bruce sounded disappointed he couldn't help on that account. "He is Hell's notary, though, so it probably is contract stuff."

"The fuck?"

Bruce nodded. "Yeah, he notarizes Hell's contracts."

"The fuck?" I felt like a broken record, but my thoughts were accurately and succinctly conveyed.

"Well," Bruce offered, "you know how archangels are all archangels of something? Michael's got paratroopers and warriors and stuff, blah blah blah, right? Well, Baalberieth was an archangel before he got the boot with Lucifer."

"So?" Gretchen asked, kicking her feet off the desk and leaning forward.

"Well, Baalberieth was the Archangel of Lawyers."

I don't know how long we sat there in silence but it lasted. "So?" I finally asked.

"Well, come on," Bruce laughed. "Why do you think all lawyers go to hell now? Why do you think lawyers get a bad rep? A bus full of lawyers goes off a cliff, what do you call it?"

Gretchen and I answered simultaneously: "A good start."

"Exactly," he chuckled. "I mean, how many millions of dollars did that idiot get suing that fast food place over getting burned with coffee now they have to put HOT on all the disposable mugs? Do you think that was the Throne's doing? That was all Baalberieth."

"So the Throne doesn't get involved with legal stuff?" Gretchen asked.

"Not often," Bruce admitted.

"When was the last time?" Gretchen persisted.

Bruce thought about it for a moment. "*Flint v. Falwell.* Jerry was being a tool and the Father decided to handwave it in Larry's favor. But he usually is a pretty hands-off deity."

"Who is Larry Flint?" Gretchen asked.

Bruce and I both looked at her with shock and surprise.

"The fuck?" I asked.

My *The fuck?* was run together with Bruce's, "Seriously?"

Gretchen nodded with all earnestness that was frankly as adorable as the circumstances were shocking.

Bruce chuckled. "The owner and publisher of *Hustler.*"

"Okay?" Gretchen asked still oddly unaware.

Bruce laughed wholeheartedly this time. "Nick can explain it later."

There was nothing I could say while Bruce threw me under that bus.

"So," he asked, "anything else you wacky kids need? I gotta bounce."

"There an easier way to get in touch with you?" I asked.

He smiled. "Yeah, call me."

"How?" Gretchen asked.

"On the phone." He seemed confused that no one was understanding the concept. "Why didn't you do that this time, by the way?"

"We didn't have your number," Gretchen confessed and shot me a look wondering if I had the number and forgot it.

I shook my head. "Hey, he never gave me his number."

Bruce reached into his inside pocket and pulled out a business card and handed it to me. It was a white card, black lettering; Patrick Bateman wouldn't have approved at all. It simply read:

Bruce Campbell (not that one)
G.A.
555-555-2662

"I thought 555 numbers were just for movies?" Gretchen asked as I showed her the card.

"It is, but it works for us, too." He smiled and stepped to the door. "Good seeing you." And then he was gone.

We looked at the card.

Gretchen scratched her head. "2662?"

I thought about it for a minute. Then it hit me and sadly it made as much sense as anything else. "Boob. 2662 on a phone spells boob."

Chapter Six

Another One of My Dumbass Plans
"Latest Disaster" Stroke 9

don't know if after the vision quest Gretchen and I went back to bed and slept. I know if we did sleep, it was only for a few hours, and the entire time I dreamed of staring at the ceiling. So I'm willing to bet I didn't sleep at all and simply stared at the ceiling. And my eyes were so fucked afterward I'm also sure I didn't blink at all. I felt a little better after splashing water on my face and drinking a can of Dr. Pepper.

There are a couple of types of people, but sometimes it's useful to narrow it down to a binary problem, *i.e. there are two types of people. Those who love the movie Krull, and those that can fuck the fuck off.* Or *there are two types of guys, those that have been to a strip club, and those that have lied about the fact they've been to a strip club.*

Well, when it comes to thinking things through and making plans, some people are screwdrivers. They can twist and turn things and wrap things around threads. Now as much as I see the value in a person that can pull off that kind of thing, that's just not really a skill set I have. I'm too shortsighted and dumbassed, I guess, for that kind of thing. What I am is a hammer: I bang nails flat and break shit.

To be fair, I know for a fact that a screwdriver person has never killed an archangel. And again, to be fair, I probably shouldn't be overly proud and brag about that.

So when Gretchen asked me, "Do you have a plan?" no one should be surprised by the dumbassery I came up with.

"We're going to the Wedge Wood, and I'm going to have a fucking conversation with Doc Douchebag Demon of Murder Archdemon of Lawyers or whatever the fuck he wants to call himself."

Gretchen mulled that over for a moment, nodding before answering slowly as she brushed a few strands of her raven hair back behind her ear. It was a sweet but innocuously seductive gesture. Were there a *How to Draw Men's Eyes* playbook, the *hair behind the ear* maneuver would be right there with the *look over the top of your glasses*.

"That's..." Gretchen bit her lip, page three of the, *how to draw men's eyes* playbook, "ballsy."

I smirked and shrugged with practiced nonchalance. "It's ballsy if it works. If I end up with my fucking head chopped off via demon ax then it'll be remembered as *reckless*, so, you know, no worse than any other plan I come up with."

Gretchen smiled, and it was like a Sweet Tart without any damned Tart. "Maybe you watched *Raiders of the Lost Ark* one too many times as a kid."

My eyes narrowed and I shot her a dirty look. In fact, I felt the Wrath jump in my guts and I focused on her to quash it. "You take that back."

She smiled and brushed her fingers over my cheek and the Wrath subsided. "I'm sorry, it's the best movie in the world."

I smiled and pulled her into a hug. We stood like that for a few moments.

"Where do you want me?" she asked quietly.

"Anyway, anywhere I can have you." I chuckled. "But today post up in the stairs and get ready to come rescue me if shit goes sideways."

She walked over and took a Craftsman tool bag from the closet then took her double pistol belt. She drew one of her custom .357 single-action Army Colts and made sure there were six rounds in the cylinder before repeating with the second.

I'd like to say we knew things would work out fine, but in all honesty, we didn't. Gretchen and I had taken it as our mantra to *hope for the best but to be ready when shit hits the fan because with us it tended to.*

I pulled on my shoulder rig and slid my 1911 out of the holster. I pulled back on the slide about half an inch and saw that there was brass. I eased the slide back forward then gently lowered the hammer before putting it back under my arm. The weight of the pistol and magazines was familiar, an eternal prop for the costume of the character of Nick in *A Tale Told by an Idiot. Full of Sound and Fury. Signifying Nothing.*

I watched Gretchen zip up the tool bag as I pulled on my suit jacket. "What do you think of hacking off a few feet of the stick so you can take the Spear with you?"

She looked to me, then to the Spear of Destiny leaning in the corner, then back to me confused. "Why don't I just collapse the staff?"

"The fuck?"

She walked over and took the Spear. I watched her fingers deftly play with something and the six-foot shaft shrunk down to one foot. She smiled and twirled the Spear tip and shortened staff like a high school majorette with her baton; to the point that she was giving an overly large fake smile and holding her other hand out dramatic to the point of dumbassery.

"How the hell did you do that?"

She smiled and twirled the shortened Spear. "It's all in the fingers and balance."

"No," I sighed, knowing I walked into that one. "How did you shrink the fucker?"

"Oh," she seemed surprised. Like someone drinking water then asking *what is this?* "Well, the Sisters in Shadow have had these bo staffs for years, easily collapsible for concealment. It's all carbon fiber and polymers and lightweight metals and—"

"Ninja shit," I interrupted. "Just say science-y ninja shit."

She flashed her smile and nodded.

Like a perv I watched her change into a pair of yoga pants, her pouch belt, a gray tank top, her Docs, and a dark green duster-looking jacket that fell to her knees. The jacket hid the two feet of collapsed Spear.

"I feel like I need a hat," she said as she looked at herself in the mirror.

"I got some ball caps in the closet," I offered, not that I thought she needed it.

"No." She bit her lip in intense concentration. "A driving cap maybe? A beret?"

"Not a beret," I said that way too quickly to get away with not explaining it. But that didn't mean I was going to offer anything either.

"Come on..." she walked over and needled my ribs. "Spill it."

"I just don't like berets."

"Didn't you wear one in the Army?" She intentionally cocked her head to the side in an effort—successful, I might add—to be cute.

"Yeah, why do you think I fucking hate berets?"

"What's wrong with them?"

"They don't keep your head warm when it's cold, don't keep your head cool when it's hot, don't keep the sun or rain out of your eyes.

They're as goddamned useless as your average fucking Frenchman in a fight against a German."

She laughed then rested her head on my shoulder; she batted those lashes as she looked up to me. "Nick, be honest, tell me how you *really* feel about berets."

I laughed, there was no stopping it.

"I guess I'll go without." She smiled and squeezed an arm around my waist.

"Good, don't want you looking too good. People will start thinking you're out of my league."

She laughed. "Sorry, but they already do."

"No, they don't, they think *Sugar Daddy situation* or, at worst, a *second family situation*."

She laughed harder. That was something. I might be handsome but not handsome enough to be with her, and mediocre in bed, but I could make her laugh. I'd also fought an archangel for her; there should be no limit to the credit on that card.

Gretchen walked out to the desk and picked up the two sets of keys. "Your car or mine?"

"How can you tell the difference?"

She flicked little tags on each with her finger. "One says *Nick,* the other says *Gretchen.* It's elementary, dear Watson."

My brow furrowed. "Shouldn't I be Holmes?"

She shook her head. "Actually, I don't think Holmes was boning Watson, even though there's plenty of shipping and fan-fic for Cumberbatch and Freeman. We're Tom Magnum and the Girl of the Week?"

I shook my head. "You're more than the Girl of the Week."

She smiled. "Tommy and Tuppence?"

I shook my head. "I read Dashiell Hammet, not Agatha Christie."

She laughed and tossed me my keys. Surprisingly I caught them and slipped them in my pocket. We locked up the office and she slipped her arm around mine and we headed for the stairs.

"You can't pull off the Tom Magnum mustache," she offered consolingly.

"I could pull off the Hawaiian shirts, though."

She nodded. "You could, but I don't think you could pull off the shorts."

I laughed. "No... I wouldn't want to try."

We walked down to the basement of the building. It'd been converted into parking and my office rent paid for four spots. One was mine, which hadn't had a car since the Miata decided to grill-fuck a telephone pole. The second was labeled for Agnes and Monday through Friday her 1970s vintage Volkswagen Bug would rest from its commute to work in preparation for its commute home. The other two spots were for customers.

Now sitting in one of the customer spots was a 1973 black Dodge Charger with white leather interior. It was an example of vehicular perfection.

"Holy crap!" Gretchen ran forward and ran her hand along the hood. "Gabby got me the *Burn Notice* Charger!"

I looked at the car in my spot, then to the muscle car for Gretchen. "The fuck?"

"What?"

"I think she got this shit backward," I said, glancing between the two cars.

Gretchen walked over and looked at the cobalt Ferrari sitting in my spot. "Why are you bitching about a Ferrari?"

"Do I seem like a fucking Ferrari guy?"

Gretchen opened the door and looked around the interior leaning back to look behind the seats. "Nick!"

"What?"

She came out of the car holding up two Heckler & Koch UMP 45 sub-machine guns. "Nick! It's not just a Ferrari, it's the Ferrari Maranello 575 with the gun case with body armor and HK UMP 45s... it's the car from *Bad Boys II*. YOU'RE MIKE LOWERY FROM *BAD BOYS II*!"

It was the dumbest damned thing I'd ever heard. "Who the fuck would think I'm cool enough to be Will Smith from *Bad Boys Two*?"

"They actually used two Ferraris for the movie. The Maranello 575 for most of the scenes, but they used the Maranello 550 for the big chase scene." Gretchen laughed and leaned back into the car to collapse the stocks on the UMPs and put them up. She stood back up with a bounce. "Well, that settles it, we're taking your car."

"Why?"

She walked over and opened the Charger's trunk. "Because unlike in *Burn Notice* the Charger isn't loaded with guns and explosives."

"Is there duct tape?"

She lifted the role and waved it before putting it back. "Well, they got that right." She shut the trunk and walked over, sliding into the Ferrari. I opened the door and plopped into the driver's seat. There might be a metaphor about me and Gretchen and the way we get into cars.

"Are you going to shoot up the dashboard like in *Bad Boys two*?" I raised an eyebrow at her.

"No," she chuckled. "I'm not Marcus. Now Jammer might have shot up the dash."

We both laughed, but it was twinged. I sometimes thought Gretchen missed Jammer more than I did. I think she missed him for me.

I got the key in and the engine literally roared into life. I'll be honest, as much as I mentally lusted over the Dodge Charger... that felt good. Really good. The tires squealed as I backed out of the spot. I was going to have to get used to how sensitive a performance car could be.

Pulling out of the parking garage with my gorgeous soulmate in a Ferrari, it did seem like I did have bigger damned things to worry about.

Chapter Seven

Fucked Up Family Tree
"Remember Everything" Five Finger Death Punch

The doorman at the Wedge Wood was the same guy Gretchen and I had staked out six months before, so I felt like I kinda knew the guy as I approached the desk. I smiled because A: people appreciate it, or B: find it really off-putting. Either way, score a point for Nick.

"Hello, I need to see Dr. Travis, Eric Travis. My name is Nick Decker, and I don't have an appointment." If it wasn't an afternoon on a weekend I would have gone to his office on the university campus. There would probably have been less of a chance for things to go sideways there. As is, I was impatient and just wanted to get this shit done.

The doorman stared at me for a moment like he expected me to hand him a business card. Business cards cost money; I'm not sure how much because Agnes takes care of that, but I knew they cost money. So the doorman of a douchebag demon academic didn't warrant one.

He finally lifted his phone and hit a few numbers. "Yes, Dr. Travis, there is a Mr. Decker here wishing to see you."

The man nodded as whoever was talking on the other end of the receiver spoke. Like the guy on the phone could see him nodding in either agreement or comprehension. "Yes, sir." He finally hung up the receiver and smiled politely to me. "Elevator is around the corner, sir. The code is four-two-one, then the floor." He said it with such a note obedience that I expected him to ask me if I wanted fries with that.

I went around the corner and hit the button for the elevator then stepped past it and into the emergency stairwell. I saw the door leading outside and could see the line of the alarm going from the door into a power box. I grabbed the line and thought about Malcolm Young passing away and Justin Bieber still being alive. My hand flared and the fire burned through the line connecting the door to the alarm.

I shook the fire from my hand and smiled. I figured either it'd kill the door alarm or set it off and force a fire alarm. Either way, it was a win-win for me. I hit the door bar with my hip and it popped open. Gretchen stepped in with a smile, looking at the burned-through line.

"What did you think of?" she asked with a genuine, as opposed to polite, curiosity.

"Malcolm Young..."

I didn't get to finish the sentence, she threw her arms around me. "Greatest band ever." How many times did I not even need to finish the sentence with her? It was weirdly comforting having someone "get me."

I nodded, the lingering anger melting away in her arms. I kissed her forehead and stepped back to the elevator bank. The doors closing as I jumped and got my hand in. I stepped inside and punched in the code and the floor then watched as the doors closed.

I knew Gretchen was taking the stairs up and would wait for shit to go sideways.

When the hell did things *not* go sideways?

I got to the floor and the elevator doors opened. There was a dark, blonde-haired lady and her eight or nine-year-old son. The kid ran into the elevator and punched me right in the left thigh. It didn't hurt, but what the hell?

I looked at the kid, then to his mom who didn't say anything. She just smiled like I should be grateful for the wonderful gift bestowed upon me by her son.

The mom stepped into the elevator and the kid hauled back like he was going to hit me again. I saw the doors starting to close. I'm not proud of what I did next, but I'm not ashamed of it either.

I hip-checked that little bastard and sent him sprawling on his pudgy little ass as I got out of the closing elevator. It didn't hurt the brat, but he cried anyway, not from pain but from not getting his way. *Mommy, I wanted to punch him and he didn't let me then he pushed me and I fell over, oh the injustice, the humanity.*

I heard the fat tears start to fall as the kid began to wail. I didn't see any of it though because I was already heading down the hall even as the elevator doors finished closing.

My smirk had nothing to do with that whiny little bastard.

Well, almost nothing to do with that whiny little bastard.

Well...

I got to the door and knocked. The last time I'd been here we'd been trying to get intel on the Spear, Switch had been here with a normal dressed Megatron, Dr. Travis had been a mortal shithead academic and Jammer had been alive waiting as backup in the van. Shit had definitely changed.

The door opened and I saw the smile bloom on the Rolf-wannabe-looking motherfucker. He held out his hand. "Nick, it's a real pleasure. Come on in."

I looked at his hand, then his eyes. "Forgive me if I do not shake hands."

His smile got even bigger. "*Tombstone,* great movie. Come on in."

I stepped inside and looked around; it still looked like the place was decorated by a douchebag. "So what do I call you? We both know the real Eric Travis is dead as the fucking dinosaurs."

He shut the door and moved past me to a bar. "Macallan, right?"

I nodded and he began pouring.

"Well, what would you suggest calling me?" he asked calmly.

"Baalberieth is a fucking mouthful," I admitted.

He smiled and turned with a glass of Scotch in each hand. "Indeed. How about Uncle Bear?"

"Uncle Bear?" If I sounded incredulous, there was a damned good reason.

"What?" He smiled as I took the glass. "Lucifer got to be Uncle Lew. Why can't I be Uncle Bear?"

"How about thirty-eight missed birthdays without a goddamned card or call? Fucker, I grew up with Lucifer around. I don't know you."

"Well, Nick, not to nitpick, but every demon in Hell is either your aunt or uncle if you think about it. Not just Lucifer."

"Lucifer earned it, motherfucker. Let's not pretend we're more than we are." I smelled the Scotch. Fuck, it smelled perfect.

"Then what are we?" Baalberieth, in the form of Doc Douchebag, seemed bemused, curious, interested.

"You're a demon, and I'm the asshole trying to figure out what you're doing here."

He smiled and clinked his glass of Scotch to mine. "Well, here's to the great existential questions."

I sipped my Scotch and glanced about. "So what are you up to?"

"Why are you curious?"

I sighed. "I just got the fucking Teutonic Knights out of my fucking city, and I get woken up this morning by a goddamned archangel who is jumpy because they can't figure out what you're doing. So I don't know when I became the goddamn emergency big red phone of this fucked up detente, but it's fucking annoying." I sipped more of the amber liquid in my probably ridiculously expensive glass. "So how about you just tell me, and I check it out to make sure you're not screwing with me, and we all walk off happy and friends?"

He patted his stomach and laughed deep and hearty. "Oh my... you know what you sound like?"

"Don't say a lawyer," I groaned. With the exception of Phil the Destroyer, I fucking hated lawyers.

He smiled and touched his forefinger to his nose and pointed at me with his hand holding his glass.

"You're not gonna make any friends saying insulting shit like that," I warned him as I finished the glass. If I ended up having to break the glass I didn't want to waste good Scotch. If only people were as good when aged eighteen years as Scotch was...

"I'm just doing some housekeeping," he assured me.

"So a dipshit summons you to clean house?" I was curious if he meant housekeeping as in: *I need to kill some people, I need to do some paperwork*, or *I need to wash the dust ruffles*.

Baalberieth chuckled. "No, he screwed up summoning me because you and yours scared the hell out of him and he thought I could help. But he really screwed the pooch, so he's gone; *voila*, here I am. And since I'm here, I had some housekeeping to do."

"Such as?"

"Well," he smiled sheepishly, "a few things."

"Any reason you don't want to drop the coy schoolgirl bullshit and just spill it?"

"I'm, not sure how to describe it. I guess the easiest and most relatable way to articulate it is...I'm not sure. Conducting a census?"

"Are you asking me or telling me?" I asked suspiciously as he took the glasses and headed back to the bar to refill them.

"Telling, I suppose." He'd probably be charming if I didn't attribute that face to a total asshat and know there was a goddamn demon lawyer under it.

"Census of who?" I was getting tired of Sisyphusing this conversation.

"Whom?" he politely corrected in a professor's lecture voice.

"Don't grammar-Nazi me."

He chuckled. "Sorry, but it is *whom*." He turned, bringing the refilled glasses back. "I think you have enough information on that subject so I think, as you would say, revert to my sheepish schoolgirl bullshit on that account. What's next?"

"You implied multiple chores."

Again, he smiled. "Did I?"

"Motherfucker..."

He laughed. "Technically, I never had a mother, simply a pure creation of the Father."

"What else?"

He sighed. "Scouting."

"Scouting what?"

He looked at me, confused. "I don't have to explain battlefield recon to you, do I?"

"What battlefield?" I felt a knot in my gut next to the ever-present fire. Like I was pre-cogging what the answer was going to be but hoping the *Minority Report* would be right as opposed to the vision.

"Armageddon." He said it plainly and flatly, utterly devoid of emotion. One plus one equals two. Two times two equals four. I'm doing fieldwork to prep for Armageddon. The southeast U.S. is humid. There are no snakes in Ireland.

I felt my teeth grind together. "I have the Fiery Sword."

He nodded. "I know. But, that doesn't mean the world can't end."

"You'll lose."

He continued nodding. "We know, but why do you think we're the ones starting it?"

My eyes narrowed. "Uriel?"

He tapped his temple with a finger as he nodded.

"Why prep if you know you're going to lose?"

He held his hands out in mock surrender; it reminded me of Lucifer. "There is losing, and there is *losing*."

"What's there to recon then?" That knot was getting tighter in my gut. At the same time, I felt the fire grow hotter. The fire I held in there that wanted to burn the world. The Wrath of God longing for The End. Capital T, Capital E. Not all caps THE END, that was just asshole-ish.

"Well, the Father set out some very specific parameters for the battlefield. Uriel is looking for a loophole."

"And Hell has its chief council looking for legal loopholes?"

He finished his second drink. "Bingo. Who better to find loopholes and close them than the most famous contract attorney ever?"

"Famous?"

He put his glass down and paced in the horribly decorated apartment. "I don't want to brag..."

"Bullshit, of course you do. Hit me."

He literally hugged himself and bounced. "I wrote the contract for the Job bet. I wrote the eviction notice for Eden AND the land grant for Nod. I did say 'Cain, why not just bash his noggin in with that lump of metal?' I wrote Noah's building and boating permits. See, as you put it, the *detente* is held together by my paper. Demon or not, both sides recognize my agreements."

"So like Faust?"

He laughed. "No, I'm not Mephistopheles. That guy is an asshole, even by demon standards, but I did write the contract."

I tried bringing us back around on task. "So, why are you still here instead of closing loopholes?"

His face, for the first time, darkened. "Because I think," he paused and gulped, as animated as a cartoon character, "I think the battle will happen here and there's nothing I can do to stop it."

Chapter Eight

Bad Reps
"Bad Reputation" Joan Jett (Yeah, I know it's obvious)

It wasn't a kick in the balls, but it was a metaphorical kick in the balls.

"Well, that fucking sucks." I finished my second glass of Scotch. I set the glass down. I couldn't afford to get too loaded right now.

"It's not the most pleasant thing in the world." Baalberieth smiled sadly. "I mean, believe it or not, I like this world. Especially after all the work Lucifer and I put into it."

"What do you mean?"

He motioned me to follow him as he stepped out onto the balcony. I followed and leaned against the door frame instead of going all the way out. He made a grand sweeping gesture out over the cityscape. "Who do you think did all this?"

I mulled it for a moment. "We did."

He smiled, like a proud professor who got the right answer out of a dip shit student. "Exactly. Now, who do you think pushed you?"

"I'm taking it the answer you're looking for is 'your side?'" I crossed my arms and felt the fingers of my right hand brush the grip of my 1911. I knew it wouldn't do a lot...I didn't really think I'd need it. It was just comforting.

"I hate to be the one to have to tell you, but the Father"—again he gestured out at the cityscape—"never wanted all this."

I cocked my eyebrows; if he wanted to monologue I'd let him. People hell-bent on pumping a monologue either gave you information they might not have needed to or just annoyed the fuck out of you. Right now there's little to lose in letting him ramble. But if I got too annoyed I was going to fucking jet.

"Look back at the Garden, or at least the representation of the Garden you were given. Adam and Eve, running around naked, picking fruit off of trees and getting by, that correct?"

"More or less."

"See, the plan was for humanity to basically be hunter-gatherers. Stay in the Garden, naked and happy, and worship the Father. And don't get me wrong, the Father is great. He's worth the worship and deserves all he gets. But here's the rub. This was my problem anyway, creating a race whose sole purpose is to worship you is a bit... needy. So in the Garden, Adam and Eve didn't know any better till Lucifer pointed the tree out. Knowledge of Good and Evil. After that, they had a choice. And isn't that better? Would you rather have someone love you who doesn't know better, or someone who understands they don't have to and does it anyway?"

I nodded. Whether I decided to buy the product, I guess I was in for the infomercial.

"So Lucifer helps them get free of the Garden. What happens next, they keep with the same hunter-gatherer BS. They pump out two kids, Cain and Abel, right? So, Abel's the big victim and Cain is history's first villain."

"Did he really bash his little brother's head in with the lump of iron that became the Spear of Destiny?"

Baalberieth chuckled. "Honestly, I'd forgotten about that. Yeah, I guess he did. But here's the rub: if you like the world, Cain is the hero."

"Wanna explain that one?"

He held up a finger. "Life expectancy in a hunter-gatherer society is shit. You look at modern Inuit tribes who subsist in a hunter-gatherer paradigm life expectancy hits somewhere around only about twenty-five percent of the population hitting age sixty. The average life span is around forty-three or forty-four. Hunter-gatherers are looking at around a twenty-five percent infant mortality rate. But here's the real shitty thing—it never gets better. Hunter-gatherers don't have hope."

"Every dumbass who is dumbassed enough to want it has hope, dude." Yes, I Just referred to Hell's top lawyer as *dude*.

"Well, yeah, in the *I hope I find food tomorrow*. But what they don't have is hope for the future. They don't have a plan to make things better for their kids. Those kids will have the same shitty life that their parents did. Abel's the hunter-gatherer. Cain was arguably the greatest human ever. He came up with farming. It wasn't Lucifer's idea, wasn't my idea. Cain freaking invented civilization."

"Okay?" I wasn't tracking. "Want to elaborate on that?"

"All right, to be fair, he never knew how it would turn out. But by definition, Cain was a better father than Abel simply because of this. Cain wanted his kids to have a better life. Abel wanted his to have the same life, so Cain invented farming. So you can argue chicken and egg, but Cain came up with farming and the idea of a surplus. That changed everything. E-V-E-R-Y-T-H-I-N-damned-G. Everything."

He walked back to the bar and opened a mini-fridge and pulled out a bottle of some craft beer. Apparently, not all the douche died with Eric Travis, colossal douche. He offered me one but I shook my head.

"So while Seth's kids were wandering hills following flocks and bloom patterns of wild fruit, Cain and his kids were building cities. Because farming is sedentary, sedentary plus surplus equals population boom. Increased population and surplus equals specialization. Seth and all his kids had to worry about not dying every day. Cain and his kids knew they weren't going to starve, so they could do other things. Frank was a farmer and grew enough that Bob didn't have to be a farmer, so Bob became a metal worker. Lisa made pottery, and on and on. It led to writing; the perpetuation of knowledge. Anything greater than tribal-level civilization is built from the work of Cain."

"Yeah." I hadn't given the subject enough thought to argue with him. "But doesn't change the fact that Cain iced his brother."

Baalberieth sipped his beer and nodded. "A sad byproduct of necessity."

"Oh, so it was necessary?"

A shadow did pass over his face, almost like me bemoaned it. "Agrarians and hunter-gatherers can't live side by side, they just can't. It boils down to resources, geography, security. So either the hunter-gatherer has to go or get killed. It's always been that way. You like the song, *Sweet Home Alabama*? You like B.B. King's, *The Thrill is Gone*? Tina Turner? Elvis? None of that would have happened had Andrew Jackson not uprooted the indigenous people in Alabama and Mississippi and forced them out to Oklahoma." He saw I was about to say something but he held his hand up to hush me. "I'm not saying it was right. I'm not saying it was good. I'm not saying it wasn't horrible. But a lot of good came from it. Know how many people died in the Manhattan Project? Does it matter? Because it ended the war. Sometimes a big evil can lead to a bigger good."

He took another long tug on his beer. I reached behind me and shut the door to the balcony figuring he wasn't going back out there.

"Had Abel been left alive, he and his would have plucked Cain's fields, taken the product of his work to get by that day. Cain was looking to tomorrow. Cain was looking forward for his kids. Sad fact is Abel had to die, Seth's kids had to be beaten and pushed out. Abraham was a nomad, and the Egyptians had built the damned pyramids. The Hebrews roamed the desert for forty years, and in the end, they built cities, the nexus of civilization. Why? Because whether they were aware of the reasons, Cain had won. And because of it, we have roads, antibiotics, beaten polio, child labor laws, art—all that is because of Cain. The Father might have sent his Son to save your souls, but if you like pizza delivery, hospitals, books, webcomics, music, good Scotch…"He paused, letting that last one sink in. "You really need to thank Cain."

He looked knowingly to me. "Plus, why should anyone have sympathy for an older brother who loves his younger brother but doesn't like him?"

"That's fucking low."

He smiled. "And if it boiled down to him or Gretchen?"

I didn't answer him. Then again, goddamnit, I didn't have to, did I?

Baalberieth leaned back against the bar. "So what's your plan, Nick?"

"What do you mean?"

"What are you going to tell Gabrielle?"

"Whatever I have to to get Switch back on his feet." I heard the steel in my voice that I honestly didn't mean to put there. But it was my fault Switch was fucked up, so it was up to me to get it fixed.

"Well, that's fair, I guess." He set his beer down and stepped toward me with his hand extended. "I kind of want to apologize to you, Nick."

"For what?"

"For trying to kill you the second I got here. I could say that going from Hell to here in the corporeal form is rough, but that would just be an excuse, and doesn't excuse. So I'm sorry about that."

I took his hand and we shook. "Sorry I hacked into you with the Fiery Sword."

He smiled, "Yeah, that did hurt like a son of a bitch." Our eyes were locked; it wasn't intimate, it was intimidating. It was like a chicken race and we were both hell-bent on not being the one to swerve first. "I can see it."

"See what?"

"What Lucifer sees in you."

Our grip dropped and I started stepping toward the door. I paused with my hand on the knob. "I'm surprised you didn't mention mom."

"Why?" He seemed bemused.

"Well, she was your sister too, right?"

He shrugged. "I hate to speak ill of the dead, but your mom was, pardon the irony, an unholy cunt. Hell for me was going to be having to listen to her prattle on for all of eternity. From what I could tell she was only loyal to three people: Lucifer, your dad, and your brother. Then again, she was insanely loyal to them." He tapped his lip with his finger for a moment. "She was like a Cleveland Browns fan longing for the glory days of Jim Brown, idiotically believing this year will be their year. How were your parents as parents?"

I shrugged. "I've seen worse ones."

"Your dad?"

I felt my head cock to the side just a bit. "He didn't know how to pick a winning pony at the races."

He laughed. "Nice allusion. Your mom? And the inequality of it all?"

"She needed a son that needed mothering. She got the shit head for that. Fuck knows he needs to be taken care of. So maybe it's not that she was a bad mother to me but that I was a shit son for her."

"That seems to be a very generous assessment on your part, Nick."

I turned the knob. "No waiter that has ever had my table would call me generous."

He laughed as I stepped out into the hall. "You are welcome anytime, Nick Decker."

I glanced back at him. "Probably not taking you up on that." I pulled the door shut and headed down the hallway to the stairs.

Gretchen waited, Spear shaft extended ready for action, pistols on her hips. She smiled as she saw me and leaned the Spear against the wall and started taking off the pistol belt and putting it back in the tool bag.

"Find out anything?"

"Hopefully enough." I picked up the bag after she zipped it.

"You okay?" she asked with a voice full of concern.

I shrugged as she started collapsing the Spear. "Apparently, I'm Cain and my brother's Abel. And it seems Cain is a fucking rockstar or something."

Her confusion was refreshing because it meant I wasn't the only one that was a little mixed up at the moment.

"Huh?" she asked tucking the collapsed Spear under her jacket.

I took her hand and our fingers interlaced as we started down the stairs. "Yeah," I nodded, "that just about goddamned says it, all right?"

Chapter Nine

Older Brothers Tend To Get Screwed In The Bible or The Number of Fucks I Give
"He Ain't Heavy He's My Brother" Neil Diamond

I gave Gretchen the cliff notes version of Baalberieth's, "Cain was a Rockstar" spiel. She took it with a quiet contemplation that reminded me of a *Jeopardy!* contestant who knew she'd nailed the *Final Jeopardy!* question but was so far behind that the point was moot. Then she started slowly nodding. "Well, you know, I've always taken the Cain and Abel story as 'murder is bad, and we have to give God acceptable offerings in the right spirit.' I never thought of it from a social evolutionary or anthropological sense."

"Okay."

She shot me a playfully dirty look. "Come on, you went to Sunday school, right?"

"Yeah," I admitted, "but not lately."

She smiled demurely. "Well, it does hold to theme, doesn't it?"

"What theme?"

"Older brothers get screwed in the Bible. In fact, if you look at the Old Testament I'm not sure there isn't an older brother besides Solomon who doesn't get hosed."

I sat my mug of hot cocoa down. "Older brothers don't get screwed in the Bible."

She raised her eyebrows in such a manner it made me wonder if she were about to ask if I could smell what the Rock was cooking.

"Okay," I said leaning back lacing my fingers behind my head. "Let's hear your case, counselor."

She bit into a scone and chewed. She wiped the corner of her mouth with a napkin. "Cain and Abel—Baalberieth made a pretty good case on that one. Ishmael and Isaac—Ishmael didn't ask for any of the bullshit and he still kinda got hosed for not being Sarah's. Esau got screwed out of a blessing by Jacob but God was cool with it. Joseph was like the youngest of eleven or twelve brothers..."

"And he was the one that got the fucking musical. I hate musicals. And the poor mother who pumped out that many kids barely got mentioned."

She nodded like a bobblehead with epilepsy. "Exactly! Then there's David, he had older brothers but God poked the finger of greatness at the youngest one, didn't he? The most beloved apostle was James, Jesus's"—she pronounced it *Hay-Seuss*—"little brother."

"*Hay-Seuss* didn't get it too bad."

Her eyes went wide and then she crossed them. "He got freaking crucified and stabbed with a spear!"

"Oh yeah..." I watched and luckily her eyes straightened out. "What about King Solomon?"

She paused and chewed her lip, then she sucked in her cheeks. "Did he have siblings?"

"I dunno." There was no reason to not be immediately honest on that one. I knew I couldn't carry that lie.

"And don't forget the whole prodigal son!" She smiled and slapped the table causing our mugs to rattle in their saucers.

I sat and stared at her and that apparently, wasn't the reaction she wanted.

"Come on!" she continued. "The younger brother takes his half of the father's stuff and whores it up while the older brother stays home, works the fields, is responsible, and does what he's supposed to do as an adult. Then little bro comes back having pissed everything all up. He didn't have an epiphany and realize *I'm hosing my life away* or *this is all wrong and I need to get on the right track*. He just parties till he's got nothing and when he's out of every other option he comes home. Crawls back, not because it's right but because he has no other choice and dad just hugs him, gives him dope threads, and throws a party. But those dope threads and the party came out of the *brother who didn't jack everything up's* half of the stuff. I know it's supposed to be a parable about the love and redemptive power of the Father, but still. It's not a great example; it's like saying, *You should be nice to people because even Hitler helped an old lady across the street*. I mean, prodigal literally means wasteful, for crying out loud."

I laughed. "Look who maxed out the non-math shit on her SATs."

She just smiled. "You know, thinking about it, you hear about the religious right in government all the time, but you don't hear about the religious left a lot. But if you think about it the Prodigal Son is basically nothing but big government socialist bullcrap."

I sat there for a second or two and just marveled at how huffed up she'd gotten. "Wow," I slowly eased into it. "Tell me how you really feel?"

She laughed and threw her napkin at me. "Asshole. You, good sir, are just deflecting."

"Did you really just say 'dope threads?'"

She giggled. "Stop it, you're still deflecting."

"How so?" If I sounded confused there was a really good reason for it.

She smiled and batted those lashes to the point that it went from sweet to diabetic. "How're things between you and your little brother?"

I felt myself bite the inside of my cheeks. "I wouldn't say they're Biblical." Maybe it was her *reiki* training but she knew where the pressure points were, didn't she?

"Little brother that mommy and daddy carried while the older brother went off and became a man? I admit it's not a perfect metaphor but it's pretty damned close, right?" She seemed pretty pleased with herself. Then her look darkened and for some preternatural reason, I had the feeling I was screwed. "I've never met your family."

"There's a good reason for that."

"Oh?" She bit the corner of her lip comically poking out the other half.

"I like you."

"And?" She crossed her arms, I wasn't sure if she was being serious or playfully dramatic. So the impending feeling of "I'm screwed" didn't go away.

"I don't like them." I didn't think the logic was too hard to follow.

"You like your nieces and nephews."

"Well, yeah..."

"Why haven't I met them?" She had me there. Point was, I would have loved to have a better relationship with my nieces and nephews. But I didn't want to put up with their parents, and that cost me the opportunity to get to play any part in the kids' lives other than as a figure in the periphery. I'd take them to the movies even though taking four kids to the movies nowadays could put a dent in the wallet—the youngest two were still too young to even realize I was a person. So that's what I was: not really a family member as much as a guy who showed up to take them to the movies. I was an uncle in the only way I knew circumstances had allowed me to be. They were never going to call to ask me for advice. I was fun-go-out-to-eat-and-go-to-the-movies guy, and that guy isn't a role model. The thought, "What would Uncle Nick do?" was never going to cross their minds. The older ones were getting to the age where college was becoming a question. I'd been to and graduated college (and a decent one at that)—their dad/step-dad hadn't—but the number of phone calls I got asking about higher education equaled the number of fucks I gave about the existential crisis facing millennials in today's ever-encompassing digital consumer environment: zero. I knew what I was to them, and I knew that was the way it had to be.

But I had never introduced them to Gretchen, or Gretchen to them.

She smiled like she knew she had me in a trap; the cat looking at the canary. "Well?"

I shrugged. "I'd rather the girls think about career options and think chemist, nuclear physicist, astronaut, jet pilot, carpenter, or motivational speaker-slash-snake oil salesman—saleswoman. I dunno what the fuck you'd call it nowadays."

"As opposed to?" Her tone sounded dangerous.

Gretchen was either going to take the compliment or get really pissed. I didn't see a third option. I shrugged and said what I was thinking anyway. Damn the torpedos. "You're too cool. You'd be the perfect Uncle Sam for the stripper community and I want to keep eating the buffet at Sharky's without having to worry about accidentally catching a glimpse of someone I know spinning around a pole or shaking daddy's little money maker for crumpled bills tucked in their undies."

Thank the Father and Uncle Lew she laughed. "That's borderline creepily sweet. Well, what about meeting your nephews?"

"You're too hot. You ponder that fact and I'll let you extrapolate the rest of the reasoning."

She sipped her coffee then her eyes went wide and she covered her mouth with her hand as she set the mug down. "Geez, coffee almost came out of my nose!"

I laughed.

"It's not funny!"

I laughed harder.

"You're a jerk," she huffed, and scowled at me so intensely that it was comical.

"Would it help you forgive me if I paid for your fucked up non-donut European pastry and coffee?" I tried to smile as sweetly as she could and failed miserably, but it made her scowl turn to a smile and she chuckled while playfully rolling her eyes.

"Yes."

I reached in my pocket and pulled out my folded in half thin wad of bills and put enough down to pay for the drinks and scones. We stood and reflexively Gretchen looped her right arm through my left as he walked down the road to the car. I'd parked it right in front of a hydrant. I could see the meter-maid—or whatever they called them nowadays, I'm getting too old to learn new terms—punching tickets out on her hand-held thing-a-ma-bob. The car behind mine had a ticket, the car in front of mine had a ticket. The Mike Lowery Ferrari. Tickets equaling the amount of fucks I give about jaywalking: *de nada*.

I held the door for Gretchen not because I was a gentleman, but because I reckoned it's what a gentleman should do. Climbing behind the wheel I could smell the leather and the *definitely making up for something* the car exuded. The engine roared into life.

"You starting to like the car?" Gretchen asked as she adjusted the controls for the built-in seat warmers.

We roared out onto the road, and I did it without managing to peel the tires again. "I would have liked the last of the V8 Interceptors a hell of a lot more."

"Well," Gretchen reached over and patted my hand on the gearshift consolingly, "if it makes you feel better I'm pretty sure this Ferrari is more expensive than a heavily modified 1974 Ford Falcon with a custom grill, roll cage, fake supercharger, and fifty-five-gallon gas tanks strapped to the back."

"Thanks." I managed to deftly weave the car through the light traffic of Sunday evening. All in all, it'd been a relatively productive day.

"Oh," she bounced in her seat. "I forgot the bomb strapped to the gas tanks, too. As cool as a booby trap would be on a car, with your luck I don't think you really need extra things that could blow up around you."

I chuckled, but it was really just puffs of air coming from my nose as my lips didn't part, but I did smirk. "You're probably on to something there."

"So, what are you thinking?" she asked as she studied my profile as the streetlight started coming on.

"Just wondering."

"What?"

"Did you fill up on scones?" I asked as I glanced over and saw her shake her head. "What do you want for dinner then?"

"Eat out or cook something back at the office?" she asked.

"I'm good for either."

She pondered for a moment. "We could stop at the store and get a couple cans of SpaghettiOs or two boxes of toasted ravioli. Which would you prefer?"

I smiled. "I got good company so I really give zero fucks about the food."

She smiled and went back to examining the car. "This thing has a CD changer."

"Anything in it?" I'd never had a CD changer. Then again I'd never had a Ferrari before either so it was a day for new things.

You know what you never hear about in the bible? The older brother's wives; most of them don't even have names. I'm not gonna go off on some feminist BS about lack of representation in the world's most popular religions, but I will say this. Anyone ever hears my story, they're gonna hear about Gretchen. She's why I'm better off than all those dudes that got the raw end of the stick in the Holy Bible.

She randomly selected a disk and a track. The speakers started blasting the heavy guitar and piano of Meatloaf's *Bat Out Of Hell*. "Well," she said what I can only describe as haunting optimism, "either Gabrielle either knows her audience or she's definitely trying to tell you something."

Chapter Ten

Sorry, We Didn't Make Enough For Company
"Youth Gone Wild" Skid Row

The office, back in the room where Gretchen and I lived, had a mini kitchen. The oven worked but the stovetop didn't. So I stood at a hot plate stirring the SpaghettiOs with meatballs in the one pot that we owned, with one of the two spoons we owned. As soon as the pot's contents were hot enough I was going to pore it equally (more or less) into the two bowls we owned. We also owned one pan, a pizza pan for oven stuff, two plates, two forks, and a butter knife we'd pass back and forth to one another. The only glasses we owned were tumblers for booze.

Behind me, I heard the simulated gunfire. "I thought you were going to play *Gears of War III.*"

"I was," she replied distractedly.

"That sounds like a Covenant plasma rifle."

"Yeah." You could hear the focus in her voice.

I watched the SpaghettiOs start to bubble again so I stirred it. "Why the plasma rifle?"

"I'm saving my energy sword."

"So you're playing the Arbiter?"

"Yep."

"So why are you playing *Halo 2* as opposed to *Gears of War III?*" I asked as I reached up into the cabinet and pulled down both of our bowls. One was a cobalt blue fiesta ware, the other was plain Coronet white. I set them down and went back to give the pot another stir.

"I don't think I can emotionally handle *Gears* right now." There was a wavering in her voice that made me want to walk over and hug her. But I also didn't want the SpaghettiOs to get stuck to the side of the pot, so I kept stirring. "How's dinner?"

"Just about done."

I smiled as I heard her call *frag out* then heard the sound of a plasma grenade exploding from the game. As capable as Gretchen was and how handy she could be in a scrap, it was easy to forget that she wasn't a trained soldier. There were things in a fight she was extremely lacking at training and experience.

Two months ago we'd ended up on the unsafe end of a scrap with a couple of dock workers. So I ended up making entry into a room unbeknownst of the fact that Gretchen had tossed in our last flash-bang seconds before. I was practically standing on it when it went off and I got knocked the fuck out. So since then, we'd been working together to get her trained in calling *frag out* if you were tossing a grenade or *flash out* if you were lobbing a banger. In movies, people would just holler *grenade,* but that was reserved for when grenades were coming at you.

I didn't hold a grudge about her rattling my noggin with the flash-bang because I knew she felt bad about enough on her own so there was really no reason for me to hold a grudge.

"So, why don't you think you can handle *Gears* right now?" I asked as I gave the pot one last scraping stir.

"I'm not ready for the Dom scene." I could hear the pain in her voice. The problem with rereading a book, rewatching a movie, replaying a video game is you know what's coming and you can't change it, no matter how much you want it to change. It leaves you with a degree of mental impotence without any kind of mental Viagra that can cure it. So instead of dealing with the emotion of the truly Epic Dom scene in *Gears III*, Gretchen had tossed in *Halo 2*. It made sense, and I respected it.

I turned the hotplate off and poured and spooned SpaghettiOs with meatballs into the two bowls. It poured more or less evenly between the two. I might have had one or two more meatballs than her, but I also had six or seven inches and sixteen years on her, too. I picked up the bowls and started walking to the bed where it was pushed against the windowed wall. I half-hopped half-plopped next to her and we used it as a place to sit since we'd ditched the old pull-out couch. I handed her the fiesta ware bowl and a sleeve of saltine crackers. The problem with saltines was you couldn't seem to buy the single sleeve anymore, you had to buy the whole box of four. The bad news was we tended to be wasteful or they'd go stale before they could all be eaten. The good news was we each got our own sleeve and didn't have to share.

Gretchen and I shared our thoughts, our bed, our bodies, our care, and cheesy enough, our love; but sharing food was beyond a goddamned line that we refused to freaking cross. She'd have her plate, I'd have mine, and never the two did meet.

"Did you get me a spoon?" she asked as she paused the game and sat the controller down.

"Shit."

She smiled. "I got it." She hopped up and sauntered across the room and came back with the other spoon. I was using the one out of the pot. "Thanks for cooking." She took a spoonful as she walked back to the bed.

Using a hand-powered can opener to open two cans of SpaghettiOs with meatballs, dumping and scraping them in the pot, heating it up, and putting in bowls was our equivalent of "home cooking." The secret was when you turned the can upside down to use the can opener to pop a hole in the bottom of the can so air could equalize and most of the SpaghettiOs and meatballs simply slide out into the pot. That trick saved me literal seconds of spoon-scraping time. Life is short.

I used my spoon to push a meatball and some SpaghettiOs onto half a cracker. Then I just popped the whole cracker in my mouth as Gretchen sat back next to me. I proceeded to use crackers as an edible utensil whereas Gretchen pushed crackers into the SpaghettiOs along the edge of the bowl letting the cracker get mostly soggy in the sauce before alternating between two spoonfuls then one cracker.

I was about halfway through my bowl when I heard a knock on the outer office door. I looked to Gretchen, she held her fist up. I sighed and did the same, we pumped them three times then she threw paper and I threw rock. She laughed and wrapped her hand around my fist and gave it a squeeze. I hopped up taking my bowl and a couple of crackers with me and headed out into the outer office and then opened the door into the hall.

He stood there in the dark blue three-piece suit with the light blue shirt, dark tie that was either a dark blue or a black—I couldn't tell—and the tan trench coat George Smiley had worn in several scenes in *Tinker, Tailor, Soldier, Spy*. His smile was genuine and infectious. He glanced at the bowl in my hand. "Catch you at a bad time?"

I finished chewing and swallowed. "I could think of worse ones."

His smile broadened. "I was hoping you'd have trousers on. May I come in?"

I stood to the side and called out. "Hey, Gretchen, Lucifer is here!"

I heard her feet hit the floor and come running into the outer office. "Lucifer. God, I've missed you." She set her bowl on my desk and ran over, giving him a hug then blushing. "Sorry about the God thing."

He gave her a squeeze. "It's all right, I'm used to that kind of thing. I think if either one of us got offended easily we wouldn't associate with Nick."

Gretchen laughed, and even though it was at my expense it wasn't mean.

Uncle Lew looked at the bowl, then me. "I really didn't mean to bother you during dinner.

I shrugged. "We had a decent day and thought we'd celebrate."

He laughed. "This is why I like you, Nick."

I shot him a confused look.

"That bowl, this evening, is why Heaven is afraid of you and those under me don't understand you." Lucifer took his coat off and hung it on the coat stand by the door. "You're incorruptible because deep down you're content."

Gretchen seemed to chew on that a minute while I finished my bowl and set it on the desk next to Gretchen's. "Nick wants things," Gretchen offered in my defense.

Lucifer smiled that ever-charming smile that seemed to light up whole rooms. "Such as?"

Gretchen started holding up a finger with each point on the list she was pulling from thin air. "Mel Gibson to get his older-guy-action-movie comeback. George Miller to finish his wasteland trilogy before he dies. Donald Glover to reboot *Beverly Hills Cop*. After that, for Hollywood to stop rebooting crap. A true-to-the-novel *Starship Troopers* movie." She held up her other hand to keep counting. "Libertarians to get their shit together, even though he knows they won't because they're Libertarians. First-class airfare for a two-week butler package vacation at Sandals Montego Bay, Jamaica—"

"Wait...how do you know about that?" I interrupted.

She giggled and shrugged. "I've been working as a private investigator for the past six months?" That got a laugh out of Lucifer.

She shook her head a bit, causing her hair to wave. "No, seriously. Since you don't look at a lot of internet porn—well, embarrassing porn anyway—you never clear your browser history."

Lucifer chuckled knowingly then looked at me. "Point is, neither side really has anything you want they can give. Meaning they can't get leverage on you, Nick. You seem to be a man with nothing to gain and nothing to lose, and that's a man who can't be controlled."

I chewed on the way he phrased that, like he knew Gabrielle had been by and I'd asked for Jammer back. Jammer wasn't coming back, neither side could, or would, do that. Jokers to the left of me, poets to the right, I guess.

"You are the distillation," Lucifer continued slowly, making sure I could keep up, "of nothing to gain, and nothing to lose. Thus, you're the big variable in everyone's equation."

"That a good or bad thing?"

His smile dimmed slightly. I might not have noticed had I not known him my entire life. "It's neither good nor bad. It simply is what it is."

There was a tonal shift in the room and we all felt it.

"So what can we do for you, Lucifer?" Gretchen asked cautiously as she walked around and sat at her desk the way she did at client meetings.

Lucifer knowingly looked to me. "So, I hear you've had a conversation with Baalberieth?"

"Yeah." I didn't want to nod, but I think I did a little. "Do we have an easier name to call him?"

Lucifer held his hands out placatingly. "He told you to call him *Uncle Bear*, didn't he?"

"Yeah, I'm not doing that."

Lucifer laughed. "Understandable, and I don't blame you on that account."

"So," I said cautiously. It's like we were all dancing around a hat with no idea what was under it. "Sorry we didn't make enough SpaghettiOs."

For an instant Lucifer laughed and I couldn't help but think of him as Uncle Lew, my dead mom's big brother. He put his hands on his knees and stood from the chair. His gaze bounced between Gretchen and myself. "I think we both know I didn't come here for dinner. But me coming here was easier than asking you out to Sheol House."

"Easier for us, anyway." Gretchen nodded in agreement. "But one is definitely nicer than the other."

"I humbly accept the compliment." Lucifer's smile was anything but humble.

"So what do you need, Lucifer? Why did you come on out this way in the first place?"

Lucifer smiled. It was sad and longing, but it was a smile. "We need to talk."

Chapter Eleven

It Didn't Come With An Instruction Manual
"My Own Worst Enemy" Lit

*W*e need to talk *is a phrase that has never led to anything good. A relative you never met died and left you millions... You've contracted a rare disease whose only side effect is your penis is going to double in size... You get to spend the evening hanging out with Freddie Mercury and David Bowie—it was just a joke, they're really not dead... We should do more anal... The tests say you should be drinking more... Ancestry.com has proven you're really fourth in line for the British Crown and as the Archduke of Some-Made-Up-Sounding-Place, you have a castle and a shit-ton of money...*

None of these have ever followed up "we need to talk."

We need to talk means you're about to lose your significant other and an overly healthy portion of your stuff.

We need to talk means you're going to have sores in a place a person really doesn't want sores.

We need to talk means you have an unplanned kid coming, or the kid you raised was actually someone else's problem.

"Hey, Fill-In-The-Name, you got a second?" means you have a promotion or bonus. *"Hey, Fill-In-The-Name, we need to talk"* means you're fucking fired.

So if you're ever in the situation where your uncle, who happens to be Lucifer, says *"We need to talk,"* you can bet your ass clenches up tight enough to turn coal into goddamned diamonds.

I waited a second to see if he'd smile and chuckle a "...just kidding," but that didn't happen. Then again, when have I ever been that lucky?

I glanced over to Gretchen—well, okay...once.

Lucifer let the W*e need to talk* hang in the air with the annoyingly patient calm of an immortal.

I finally broke the thick silence with the equivalent of a Shakespearean sledgehammer. "Okay?"

"How was your conversation with Baalberieth?" His tone was off-handed. The problem with picturing your uncle, the capital-D Devil, as the most skilled and subtle actor of the 20th and 21st centuries combined, is he can say a whole lot with an annoying little.

"Yep." I walked over and plopped behind my desk. I reached in the drawer and pulled out two tumblers and the rapidly depleting bottle of the Macallan.

"He still on his 'Cain was a great man' kick?" Lucifer leaned forward with his elbows on his knees and fingers delicately intertwined.

"More or less." I poured two fingers into each of the tumblers before corking the bottle, then seeing how little was left I just poured the rest into the two glasses. I popped the cork back into the empty bottle and tossed it at the trash can by Agnes's desk. It missed with a thud and clattered back against the wall behind her chair.

"Well, the bad news...I believe Uriel is going rogue." Lucifer nodded his thanks as he took the tumbler.

"There any good news?" I clinked my glass to his.

"You're no worse off than you were yesterday." His manner was comforting, but I'll be honest, that bit of information wasn't comforting at all.

"So, what do we do?" Gretchen asked as she took her feet off the desk and leaned her elbows on it instead.

"Well..." he shifted in the seat and for the first time in my life, I saw Uncle Lew as what I could only call, uncomfortable. "The long-term solution is to protect the Wrath by getting it away from Nick."

"Wait," I said, half-angry the other half-confused. "That's been a goddamned option?"

"Well..." Lucifer shifted in the chair again.

"We could just give it to the Dalai Lama!" Gretchen burst as she bounced excitedly in the chair. I must have shot her a confused look. Her eyes were wide as she shrugged. "Well, we don't want to give it to the Pope. He'd just give it to an archangel. But why should the Dalai Lama care? He's freaking zen."

"For starters, he's old," I offered. "Like really old. FDR gave him a watch, for crying out loud." I glanced at Lucifer. "Right?"

"That's true." Lucifer nodded in agreement. "Plus, even if you gave it to the position of the Dalai Lama and not just the person of the thirteenth..." He paused. "No, sorry, fourteenth Dalai Lama. Anyway, the next Dalai Lama will be chosen by the Pancham Lama, who has more or less been the hostage of the Chinese government for years now. So the next Dalai Lama is more or less going to be a puppet of the Chinese state."

You could see Gretchen chew the inside of her cheek before asking, "And why's that a particularly horrible thing?"

"They're communists," I offered, and Uncle Lew nodded in agreement.

"So?"

"A good communist," Lucifer offered, "even if most Chinese nowadays are bad communists, but regardless, a good communist is, for lack of a better term, evangelical. Evangelical politically, not religiously. Regardless, I wouldn't want any evangelical, regardless of creed, to wield the Wrath of God."

"So a Muslim is out, right?" I said.

Lucifer laughed. "I'm sure any *Twelver Shia* you gave it to would instantly be proclaimed the *Mhadi*."

"Huh?" Gretchen grunted. It was odd seeing her lost in a conversation considering she was more or less smarter than me.

"*Twelver Shia*," Uncle Lew said.

"Iran more or less," I interjected.

Lucifer nodded and continued where I left off. "...Are more or less praying for a mythical figure called the *Mhadi* to come and lead them and bring about the end of the world."

I added, "It's some real Frank Herbert *Dune* shit that they're downing with the intensity of a Scientologist masturbating to *Battlefield Earth*."

That got a laugh out of Lucifer. "Sadly, giving to Wrath to just anyone is out of the question." Then his eyes fell solely and intensely on me. "But you could give it to a child."

Uh-oh... "You mean like an orphan kid?"

He shook his head no.

Shit... "Or some stranger's kid?"

He shook his head no.

Goddamnit... "So what are you saying."

He shrugged his shoulders meekly like he was trying to sink his head into his torso like a turtle. His voice matched the physicality of his action at that moment perfectly. He gestured between Gretchen and me. "Well, if you two—"

Our hands shot out like a crossing guard. "You can put that on pause," Gretchen interjected.

Simultaneously a, "Oh, *hell* no!" erupted from my lips.

Lucifer held his hands up in surrender. "I didn't think it was a viable plan either, but I don't want you walking off with bad information."

"What do you suggest?"

"Well, as it stands," Uncle Lew said with a sad tone, "if you die, the Wrath goes up for grabs. Before, neither side could find your mother, so the world was safe. You, Nick, are deemed uncontrollable, so the world is safe. If a known quantity had the Wrath, that would be the end of things."

"That doesn't sound like a suggestion."

He chuckled. "You're right, it's not. So the best I can offer is for you to keep the Wrath out of anyone else's hands."

Gretchen's features darkened suspiciously. "You keep saying it like that. Why?"

"Like what?"

"The Wrath, not the Sword."

He paused, thoughtfully for a moment. "Well, it's the more accurate of the descriptions."

"How so?" I started feeling cautious. I didn't like it when Uncle Lew got technical in his details.

He lazily waved his hand. "Well, all pistols are firearms, but not all firearms are pistols."

I instantly chewed on that. I'd used the Sword as a one-handed affair and had it instantly shift into a two-handed deal. "So you're saying it could be any kind of weapon I want?"

"Somewhat. It isn't a range weapon. You can't project it beyond your grasp, so you can't make it the pistol Painless from *Hellboy*." He smiled as if this were something I should have known, like telling a kid to not put his finger in another kid's nose. "But any kind of hand weapon—sword, knife, club, flail, whip..." He twisted his finger as he listed them off. "Really anything you'd find in the melee section of a *Dungeons and Dragons* manual before the fourth edition."

Gretchen's eyebrows almost came together. "Why just versions one, two, and three?"

"*And* version three-point-five," Lucifer added as he chuckled to himself. "Oh, Gary Gygax was alive for those; after he died my people stepped in. All those moms who thought their kids were worshiping the devil while playing *D&D* wasn't true until the fourth edition." He shrugged his shoulders and sipped his scotch.

"So you're saying I could be Indiana Jones-ing shit with a whip made of fire?" I could see the image in my head and knew it was cooler than any reality would be. I could barely deal with the Sword. I'd end up fucking myself up with a whip.

Lucifer smiled. "You could, I guess, but you'd have to start carrying a custom Smith and Wesson 1917 Hand Ejector cut from a six-inch barrel to four, as opposed to your normal 1911."

Gretchen reached over and patted my hand. "You could pull off the hat."

"Just remember, Nick, it's a weapon, but it's also a shield. You know it's made you stronger, tougher, *et cetera*, and it also functions as protection for you." Lucifer paused to let that sink in.

I thought about all the near misses I've had since all this bullshit started. I thought about Zadkiel kicking me through that window. Apparently, the Wrath of God was enough to save me, but Jammer was still dead...Switch was still fucked up.

I grabbed my phone and thumbed through the contacts that Agnes kept updated and shot a text. Not twenty seconds after I hit send there was a knock on the door. Lucifer looked over to it with a raised eyebrow that oozed bemusement.

I got up and walked around the desk to the door. I opened it with a smirk and Gabrielle stood there in a light blue vest and matching skirt with a white silken blouse. The hallway fluorescent lighting made her golden hair shine; I wasn't sure if it was an accident or not, with the illusion of a halo. Her blue eyes went wide as they fell on Lucifer sitting in the chair sipping a Scotch.

Again, Lucifer smiled and raised his glass slightly in salute to the lady archangel at the door.

"Baalberieth is taking a census and trying to figure out what the fuck Uriel is up to." I didn't see a reason to fuck around at the moment so I just got to business.

Gabrielle obviously decided to not fuck around either. "Census of what?"

"Nephelim," Lucifer threw out there offhandedly before adding in a friendly but slightly chastising tone. "You could have just asked me you know instead of bothering Nick about it."

Gabrielle's eyes darted from Lucifer to me as I demanded. "Now, fix Switch."

Back on the desk, my phone rang.

Gabrielle's eyes were locked to mine as if we were in a having a staring contest and the loser had to do the other's taxes. The phone kept ringing and behind me, I heard Gretchen's voice.

"Hello?" There was a pause. "Nick...it's...it's for you." She waited a second. "You need to take this."

I stepped backward, keeping my eyes locked on Gabrielle. I didn't break the look until I took the phone and glanced at it. The contact showing was Saul's Pistol and Pawn. I put it to my ear. "How's it hanging, Yuri?"

The voice that answered wasn't Yuri's. The voice was soft and feminine, but feminine in the way that a brick wrapped in a silk scarf and used to bludgeon someone with was feminine. "Sorry to disappoint, Mr. Decker."

"Who the fuck is this?" My voice had gone frigid. Uncle Lew was standing, setting the glass down, face full of concern. Gabrielle stepped into the office and shut the door, face full of worry.

I heard the galvanization of hate and desire even through the phone. "Uriel."

Chapter Twelve

Racing The Clock... In a Ferrari...
"Winterborn" Cruxshadows

The song started with heavy guitars and driving piano beat before slowing and the operatic voice of the singer beginning *The fires are burning and the engines are howling way down in the valley tonight.*

The tachometer jumped into the red and the tires peeled and I didn't care that the Ferrari fishtailed coming out of the parking deck and onto the street. Gretchen sat next to me with her revolvers strapped to her thighs. My .45 was under my arm and Jammer's nickel-plated Kimber was stuffed in the back of my pants under my jacket.

Lucifer told me it was a trap. Gabrielle had agreed with him. Gretchen had assumed it as a matter of fact. I had zero fucks to give.

Uriel was at Saul's Pistol and Pawn.

Lucifer had told me to run. Gabrielle had again agreed with him. Gretchen had my back. Yuri had had my back and now he and Mary Jo were in a shitstorm. Switch had had my back and he'd been laid up in the hospital for six damned months. Jammer had had my back and now he was dead. I knew I should have ran…

Because the fate of everything was sitting squarely on my shoulders.

Academically, I understood that.

But the other more subtle voice whispered in the back of my head, *A man's got to stand for something.*

I dropped from fourth gear to third as I drifted around the corner from Fifth onto Main and slammed the throttle, clutched back into fourth and quickly into fifth as I threaded the car between a beer truck and a mid-sized economy car. I made the yellow light but wouldn't have stopped for the red regardless.

What did I stand for? I wasn't in the Army anymore. I had gotten out when the shit that shouldn't matter seemed to matter more than the shit that should. If I were honest, I didn't give a rat's ass about other people's John Lockeian rights of life, liberty, and property.

I could feel the Wrath in my gut wanting to break free and burn the world, and there was an overly large segment in the pie chart of my mind reading: *fuck it, world has it coming.* I would look at humanity and see an at worst, "brutal", and at best "worthless" shitshow that I just couldn't seem to find a care to give about whether it starved, flooded, or burned.

Yet as apathetic as I was, I knew exactly what I had to stand for. Yuri had sniped from a rooftop, killing Heaven's Hotdogs because I'd needed help and he'd had my back. Switch was laid up because he had had my back. Gretchen sat next to me hurtling toward a confrontation with an archangel because she had my back. Jammer was dead because he had had my back.

What did I have to stand for? The fucked-up family I'd found along the way. There was a responsibility to stick your ass in a crack for the people who were willing to stick their ass in a crack for you.

Had I ran, it would have been better for everyone. Lucifer and Gabrielle both knew and pointed this out. Gretchen knew this and yet she was hurtling into the shit with me into a situation that would be, as Jammer once said, *dick-deep in stupid.*

We jacked my phone into the radio. It didn't have Bluetooth as it was a 2005 car and the radio hadn't been upgraded. Over the speakers we were playing the only song I could figure was appropriate for the moment. *O Fortuna* We might as well have been on an Arthurian quest for all the hope we had. And at the same time we'd had hope. To be fair, I had fought an archangel before and won. The bad news was I was still the only person ever to have done so.

"Do we have a plan?" Gretchen asked as her head bobbed in time with the music. As heart-pumping and violence-inducing the tune was, we had no idea what the operatic voices were saying, thus singing along would have felt odd.

"Same as last time." I sped past a cop car without a damn bit of notice or response.

Gretchen looked at me incredulously, even though I wasn't paying attention because I was trying to not fucking kill us as I drove. "You had a plan the last time?"

"Kinda," I said, tearing past a Smart Car.

"'Kinda' isn't the most inspirational of words, Nick." In a world falling to shit, Gretchen tried to keep things light. She was too good for me.

"Kinda sorta?" I offered.

She laughed, and that helped. "What are you thinking?"

I glanced at her then back to the road. The streetlights we passed casting shadows across her face, which was partially lit by the interior controls of the Ferrari. "I'm thinking that no matter what I do, at best this gets messy and at worst the people I give the most shit about could end up dead."

"Don't think about it." She reached down and put her hand over mine on the gear shift.

"Little hard not to." I dropped from fifth to third gear and cut a wide arching turn putting us onto Shoreline Drive.

"Nick," she said slowly, like she was looking for the right words and elongating each letter to buy time. "You are at your best when you're not thinking."

"Uh, thanks?"

She squeezed my hand on the shifter. "What I mean is, some people are thinkers. Some people think so much that they never get anything done because they're too busy thinking and wondering what could go wrong. Some people don't make decisions. They just drag things out till circumstances make the decisions for them. Neither of them are you."

I wanted to say, *No, I'm the guy that gets his friends killed in circumstances where both Heaven and Hell have decided to fucking tag team me like a cheap Nick's First Fire-Spit Fuck Session porno*, but I didn't. Her insane optimism was comforting, even for a cynic like me.

"So if we don't have a plan, do we have something like bullet points, a vague outline, a riff...or are we Indiana Jones'ing the whole thing?" She pulled one of her revolvers and checked all six cylinders before holstering it and drawing the next to do the same.

"You're going to get Yuri and Mary Jo clear." I passed a Porsche whose driver thought we were going to make a game of this. But he wasn't willing to push his German machine as much as I was willing to push my Italian one. His license plate had read, FKURMOM, so I lept to the assumption of a great quality human being there.

"What about you?" There was concern in her voice. She already knew about me, but was really hoping I'd say something other than the obvious.

"I'll deal with Uriel." This wasn't a pastry, so there was no reason to sugar coat it.

"So, you're going with the Indiana Jones plan again?" She holstered her second pistol.

"Stick to what works, right?" I flashed her a smirk I secretly hoped seemed way more confident than I felt. We parked a block back and over from Saul's Pistol and Pawn. I took Jammer's 1911 from the back of my pants and thumbed the hammer back. Gretchen had the collapsed Spear in her left hand and one of her custom .357s in her right as we ran down the road.

We saw two college girls dressed like fucking targets for the part of town they were stumbling through, drunk. I ignored them as we jogged past, having bigger things on my mind and all.

But Gretchen turned her head and gave them a chipper, "You have forgotten the face of your Father." I tossed her a confused look and she gave an exasperated sigh. "Nick, you need to read more Stephen King."

"I read *The Shining*."

"You liked the movie better, didn't you?" She was mocking me, I could tell.

We slowed to a walk as we approached the back door to Saul's Pistol and Pawn. "Yep." I grabbed the knob and thought about the shitty naive life choices of the girls we'd passed and gave the door a yank. The Wrath gave me strength and I tore open the door, bringing a section of the frame with it.

I entered first with Gretchen checking our six before rolling in behind me. We moved down the hallway and I kicked open the door that led into the store, putting us behind the counter.

Whatever it was came at me in a blur before Gretchen could even get out of the door. It tore me over the counter and I grabbed what turned out to be a wrist, dragging the blur with me as we crashed through a drum set and into a stand, bringing down several guitars that had been left at the Pistol and Pawn by dreamers who had awakened to reality.

She was above me, both hands at my throat as her bright red hair cascaded into my face. I reached up and grabbed a handful of hair and punched where I guessed a face should be with all the strength the Wrath would muster. The first punch did a little, the second did a little more, and the third caused the grip at my throat to loosen enough for me to breathe.

Gretchen vaulted the counter and thrust with the now extended Spear. The ginger above me let go of my throat with one hand and twisted, grabbing the shaft of the Spear as it passed where her side had been only a second ago. I glanced at the Spear tip between us and was happy that had it gutted me it would have only been stomach, liver, kidney, and intestine that would have been jacked up instead of my junk.

The ginger twisted her arm, trying to wrench the Spear free but Gretchen kicked out using her *aikido* or *jeet kune do* or just idiot reflex and caught the ginger in the back of her elbow, causing her to drop the Spear.

I tugged her hair and bucked my hips hard enough to drag her off me and she rolled onto the floor as I tried to get my footing.

I got to my feet just in time. The ginger did one of the flying leaps Zadkiel had tried to use on me at Gretchen, but I got her by one arm and by her belt and pivoted, throwing her through the large pane window at the front, through the bars, and into the street.

Yuri and a visibly frightened Mary Jo came out of the locked gun room where they'd been hiding. I grabbed Jammer's Kimber off the ground and tossed it to Yuri, then looked to Gretchen and told her with surprising calm, "Go on, babe, I got this."

Gretchen had Yuri lead the way and she took up the rear. I stepped into the gun room and grabbed a double-barrel shotgun off the wall. I don't know if I was guided to it or if I'd just grabbed it at random. I heard horrific screaming out on the street and figured it was the ginger. I loaded the Stevens 1960s vintage side-by-side double-barrel with double-ought buckshot and stuffed shells into my pockets. I stepped back into the storefront and looked out to the road.

The ginger pulled her hair from her face. She had high angular cheeks but a weak chin. She was pale as porcelain and was offset by the red leather jacket she wore zipped to the throat and black leather pants. Three things stood out. First, her hair floated and danced like it was made of fire. Second, she held a glowing sword of light in her right hand. Third, wings had sprouted from her back, each one as long as she was tall, so both about five-and-a-half feet. Uriel's eyes burned as bright as her blade so that they were like looking into LED lights.

She screamed the same horrific scream I'd heard a second ago in challenge.

I started stepping toward the shattered window and I let go with the Wrath. I thought about what Lucifer had told me. It wasn't a Sword it was a weapon.

I watched my right hand wreath and become encased in fire. I watched a long, wide, rounded end blade extend from it. I lifted it and the blade formed teeth of fire and they began to whirl with a roar of a two-stroke motor. I held up the double-barrel shotgun and used the whirling blade to cut it down to an illegally short length. Over a foot of the two steel barrels fell to the concrete with the *ping clink* of falling metal.

I stepped out of the broken window onto the sidewalk, double-barrel sawed-off in my left hand, a chainsaw of fire encompassing my right.

I smiled. Bruce Campbell would be pleased.

"All right, She-Bitch, let's go."

Chapter Thirteen

Come Get Some
"Wasted Years" Iron Maiden

You sometimes notice weird shit in life-and-death situations. As she did the crazy angelic flying jump at me her blade was pointed straight forward like her goal was to skewer me. Instead of blocking it with my fiery chainsaw hand I raised the sawed-off 12-gauge and shot her sword made of light and charged forward obliquely to the left. Her sword was knocked off target and I ducked under her white and golden wing as I slashed up with the roar of the fiery chainsaw ripping along, it tearing off chunks of giant feathers, which smoldered and disintegrated like burning tissue paper floating up into the air. That was when I noticed the oddly surreal fact that she was barefoot.

Her wounded wing seemed to crumple in on itself, and she landed outside the broken pawn shop window. She spun and a shield of light materialized on her left arm. She spun and lashed out with her non-injured wing and her long, thin rapier-like sword. My fiery chainsaw roared and I swung it in an overhead arc as I let fly with my remaining shotgun barrel. The double-ought buck knocked the blade off-target as I blasted her hand. The fiery teeth of my chainsaw hand tore into her left wing. I put all my strength into it and let the teeth dig in. There was no blood, only sparks of light. I was so intent on trying to cut that damned wing off I didn't notice her shield plant into my shoulder and damned near knocked me over.

Even as I stumbled I thumbed the barrel catch and breached the shotgun. I hooked it over my right forearm and tugged out the two spent shells. My Wrath of God Spider-Sense told me to duck so I didn't question it. I dove forward and somersaulted forward. Then I instantly rolled to the right while tugging two shells out of my pocket and slid them into my side-by-side shotgun. I pushed up to my feet. I closed the shotgun breach with a flick of my wrist and faced her as she came at me.

Her wings were gone like they'd de-materialized or sucked back in her body or something. I didn't have time to ask questions as I brought my fiery chainsaw around to parry her rapier. In reality, there was no way I could whip a real chainsaw around as fast as I was, but the good news was the Wrath of God is basically weightless.

Her eyes burned like the bits of phosphorous that broke off a star cluster flare. Unlike Zadkiel, her outfit's basis was economy of motion as opposed to looking like a purple-clad celestial pimp. Her shield dematerialized and was replaced by a three-bladed, blade-breaker dagger. Her form was so perfect in her attacks I half expected her to tell me, My name was Inigo Montoya you killed my father, prepare to die. The only thing that was keeping me in the fight was the skill imparted to me by the Wrath, idiocy, and sheer fucking balls.

Her attacks were relentless. It wasn't like in a movie where the fighters come together in a clash then break, pause, and attack again. She came at me again and again without respite or hesitation. We ended up moving down the street away from the Pistol and Pawn. Fighting under the glow of the street lights, even though had it been total darkness, she created enough light with her eyes and weaponry to illuminate a freaking stadium.

I sidestepped a thrust and saw her drive three-quarters of her blade through the hood of a car and into the engine block. I brought the whirling blade of the fiery chainsaw down on the blade and tried to drive it up to her hand, but it was stopped by the light blade's guard. She stabbed the breaker blade forward and hooked the bar of the chainsaw. I felt her trying to rip it from how it encased my hand.

I wasn't sure she could rip the Wrath of God from me, but I wasn't changing it. I pushed sawed-off barrels of the shotgun to the side of her head, right against her ear, and gave her both of them, point-blank. Her head rocked to the side and she stumbled away from me. Zadkiel had said at best gunfire was a bee sting. But a bee sting to the ear, I was pretty sure anyway, would fuck up anyone. On top of that a shotgun shell didn't let loose one bee sting, but a fucking hive's worth.

I quickly breached the shotgun over my arm and reloaded as I kept my eyes locked on her. She slowly regained her equilibrium while I caught my breath. She glared at me with her glowing eyes and let fly that soul-cracking scream.

"Fucking Christ, lady…" I sighed and flicked my wrist to close the breach of the boom stick. "Are you not even going to monologue or anything?"

I watched as the breaker blade and rapier in her hands melded together and morphed in a blur of light into a double-bitted ax. Maybe it was obscure trivia in the back of my head or it was the Wrath telling me it was a labrys.

I breathed heavily and slowly exhaled. "Okay. Okay…" I motioned with the shotgun and rolled my head on my shoulders. I was a little disturbed by the wrapping paper crinkle sound I heard as I rolled my neck then my shoulders. I looked to the glowing-eyed archangel. "Come get some."

With the rapier, her attacks had been staccato jabs and quack batting parries. Her entire form exuded economy of motion, in a lot of ways a minimalistic force. Not that she wasn't trying to kill me, but that she was trying to burn as little energy as possible in the ending of my miserable life.

With the labrys, that changed. She didn't chop with it as much as she gave arcing sweeps of the curved cutting edges of the ax. One fore sweep turning into the returning back sweep. One motion blending into another. Each pass of the labrys left the illusion of a light streak in the way a kid's glow stick did when waved around. Hers weren't the hard chops of a lumberjack; she was dancing a bladed ballet of which the finale would be me dismembered or fucking dead.

Sparks of fire and light showered around every time our weapons clashed together. She was driving hard with her whirlwind attack until we were fighting in the middle of a three-way intersection of the road we were on and an alley to the right. This was the first time she'd broken off in the attack.

We were still close, only three feet beyond the reach of our hand weapons. Her eyes dimmed and I started reloading the double-barrel shotgun that I had discharged again in the fight. I was nowhere near as quick at reloading it as Ash Williams appeared to be.

"Tired?" Her voice was far more pleasant than it had been on the phone.

"Now you're going to monologue?" I got the fresh shells in the barrels.

"No." She smiled, and it was utterly without warmth. "But you did forget what your military taught you."

"Bitch, I've forgotten pretty much anything anyone has taught me." As comebacks ran, it wasn't my best or most self-complimentary, but I was fucking tired.

There was a flash of light behind me that flashed my shadow down the road. Then there was a flash of light from the alley. I half-turned putting the shotgun toward Uriel as I looked. There were two, identical-looking men dressed in white turtlenecks, pants, shoes. Both men were bald but wore gold bands around their foreheads. They both drew short swords of light.

I sighed. "Motherfucker…" I looked at Uriel. "This where you tell me to give you the Fiery Sword?"

She shook her head. "I'll simply take it from your corpse. It'll be in my possession before you even get to Hell."

I felt myself shake my head. "So what did I forget?"

She gently cocked her head slightly to the side as if she were trying to figure out if I were kidding or not. "Maintaining a three-hundred-and-sixty-degree situational awareness and security?"

"Oh," I chuckled. "That. Well, never tell me the odds." I started charging at the angel in the alley. If I could kill him quickly, that would give me either a place to run or at least funnel both the other enemies into one lane. I had thought *what would Han Solo do?* but pulling my pistol and blasting would have just ended up with angels pulling a Darth Vader and landing all the rounds on their hand to no good effect. So, sadly, this seemed the best plan.

I got in the alley before the other two got to me, but I knew they were closing. They all seemed surprised by my movement like they'd just expected me to stand in the road and take it like a punk bitch. The angel readied his blade, and I didn't pause in my running. I shot his blade hand with the shotgun, causing his entire arm to fly wide. I stepped to the free side and half-lept, half-sprinted forward while lashing out with the Fiery Chainsaw. I felt the flame teeth bite but keep spinning. My feet planted and I half-turned dragging my blade arm forward. All of a sudden it came easy as the angel's head fell off his shoulders, having had his neck chainsawed through.

I turned and got the sawed-off shotgun up just in time to let the second barrel loose six inches from Uriel's rage-filled face as she moved to swing the labrys. I must have caught her in her eyes because she reached up grabbing her face with her free hand as her head snapped back from the shot.

The headless angel flashed in a soundless explosion of light but did no physical damage. But it did teach me a lesson. I saw the reaction on the remaining angel's bland face. Want to know who is afraid of dying? An immortal. The angel instantly locked up, unsure what to do, powerless in the face of proof that there could be an end to a being, which up to that moment had wholeheartedly believed itself to be timeless.

To my utter shock, the action he decided to go with was to run. He put his back to me and sprinted away as fast as his legs would carry him. He turned the corner back onto the road and I saw the flash of light. I was really hoping that flash was him teleporting away and not him saying *Sup?* to his buddies who had just shown up.

I turned and saw Uriel pulling herself to her feet, her face contorted with rage. I threw the empty boomstick at her and, like Superman, she dodged out of the way. They can take the bullet, no sweat. Slam a knife into their chest and let the blade crumple, no problem. Smile as they're punched...easy. But you toss something at them and Superman and archangels get the hell out of the way.

I watched the wings appear from her back. They beat once and I felt the gust of air. But I reached out and grabbed the wingtip. I had a good grip and I used all the strength the Wrath could give me I yanked. It started pulling her out of the sky but she swung her labrys and I barely got the Fiery Chainsaw up in time to block it. I had to brace my forearm with my other to even soak the impact. The air beat down on me and Uriel took off into the night sky.

I was alone in the alley, the only evidence of our fight was a sawed-off shotgun on the ground and an inch-wide gold band, which used to be a halo, laying on the concrete.

Chapter Fourteen

The Problem With Speeding Across Town In A Ferrari
"Here I Go Again" Whitesnake

The halo was heavier than I thought it'd be, but then again it was—probably anyway—solid gold. I slid it over the barrel of the shotgun and carried the weapon over my shoulder. A shotgun sawed off that short was easily worth ten years in prison, but I was keeping it anyway. The problem with that was hopping in a bus was out of the question, and the one Uber I summoned with my phone sped away when the driver saw it, so zero stars for that asshole.

This lack of options left me walking.

I hummed White Snake's *Here I Go Again* as my Chucks carried me across the sidewalk. I was sticking to side streets and alleys to avoid any cops, do-gooders, or Imperial entanglements. I kept glancing about for something to hide the sawed-off in but kept coming up nil.

I didn't really have a plan for the halo, but it seemed stupid to leave it there. I kept glancing up, expecting Uriel to pounce on me like a hawk going after a barn cat. Finally, in an alley I found a bit of old carpet. I tore it and wrapped the sawed-off boomstick in it with the halo. After that, I looked like a guy carrying around a fucked up bit of carpet as opposed to a guy carrying around a felony.

I stopped on the sidewalk and leaned my odd parcel against a wall before fishing my flask from my pocket. I wasn't going to say I *needed* a drink, but I definitely *wanted* a drink. I screwed the cap off the flask and took a long slow pull of Macallan. I let it sit in my mouth tingling over my tongue before swallowing with a slight shudder before it got too warm in my mouth. I thought about it then took another. With the cap screwed back in place, I slipped it back in my pocket and started walking.

My hands tucked in my pockets I got about forty feet before I turned around and jogged back to pick up the carpet bundle that I had left against the wall. I stepped back off with a purpose, not that I had any idea what to do next. I knew from Baalberieth that Uriel was reconning but I had no idea what. Six months ago this is when I would have called Jammer. Now that option was worth as much as a fart in a tornado. With Jammer dead and Switch laid up, Gretchen off with Yuri; my bench was pretty damned thin.

I saw a bus stop up ahead and thought about getting a ride but thought about the rolled-up bit of carpet with the shotgun. Really, I just needed to think, and walking was good for that.

The gas station was quiet that time of night; the disinterested clerk didn't even look up from behind his bullet-resistant glass as I stepped inside. I pulled a Dr. Pepper from the cooler and a package of bungee cords and a light cargo strap from the aisle where you could get generic wrenches and motor oil. I carried them up to the counter and put them in the drawer. The guy didn't take his eyes from the TV as he pulled the drawer back and rang me up. I dropped a ten-dollar bill into the slot that reminded me of a peep show, but instead of a few minutes of fantasy I was getting something tangible.

I went outside and put the carpet bundle on top of a newspaper machine and wrapped the bundle up with the bungies. Then with the strap, I rigged up a sling strap and tossed the whole thing over my shoulders. I stuffed my right hand in my pocket and carried my Dr Pepper in my left, sipping from it every few steps as I started ambling down the sidewalk back toward the office.

I figured Gretchen would end up back at the office eventually. Then it dawned on me that I could call her and see what was up. Unlike her, I was old enough to remember when cell phones weren't an everyday thing. I remembered the world of high school—kids showing off their pagers and setting them on the hoods of cars and letting them race on the vibrate setting. I started to pull my phone out then remembered she had a phone, too. She could just call me, so if she wasn't calling maybe she had a damned good reason for it. I kept my hand in my pocket, I sipped my Dr Pepper, and I kept walking.

My brain went back to the lack of intel problem. It dawned on me, what good would knowing do anyway? If Uriel was—mind the phrasing—hellbent on kicking off the end of the world, what the fuck could I do about it? What could anyone do? If she'd found a local place suitable for the end of the freaking world could I make it unsuitable? Get Lucifer to stack the place with demons or shit to rob it of any tactical value? That option was predicated on me knowing where shit was going to go down. That looped me back around to having a thin fucking bench; the ouroboros of bullshit in my life.

I turned the corner and groaned as I saw a few hookers working the block. Hookers are strippers who had given up on their dreams. I prefer strippers. At the same time, where you found hookers you found pimps nearby, and pimps were pains in the ass. I had to deal with pimps in the P.I. game. Easiest way to find out if a client's husband was cheating on her was to find where he was finding his girls. It was either someone he already knew or he was hiring pros, and that meant finding the pimp and handing some cash over for info about the next time the mark calls. Most pimps are scumbag pieces of shit, and they treat their girls exactly how you'd expect them to. But here's the thing...do those girls deserve better? Probably. Is it my job to save them? No. An alky will tell you, "God, grant me the serenity to accept the shit I cannot change, the courage to change the shit I can, and the wisdom to accept the fucking difference." I could spend my days trying to bust up every asshole who gave a working girl five across the face, and you know what? It wouldn't make a fucking difference. It's warning labels on packs of cigarettes. No girl goes into that game not knowing the bullshit involved. Yet for some reason or another, they go into it. I never met a working girl that wasn't a sad story, and at the same time I never met a working girl that wasn't there for a reason, and at the end of the day, they chose to be there.

I got all the sympathy in the world for a wife whose hubby beats her once. I don't have the time of day for a lady whose hubby beats her twice. She knew what she had and stuck with it. Does it suck? Sure. Do I care? No. Because what good would caring do? I got problems making rent; I got Gretchen and Agnes relying on me to bring in the bacon. At the end of the day, I'm just the Devil's nephew, not the Son of God. It's not my job to save anyone, and yet because of the Fiery Sword, it was up to me to if not save everyone, to at least keep this freaking world turning.

I glance at the working girls and pondered the irony that their problems are too big for me to fix, and yet here I was trying to avert Armageddon. I could send them "thoughts and prayers", but let's be honest, T&Ps were just mastubatory. They might make you feel good, but don't really do shit. Nothing's accomplished. Self-gratification is just selfish. Better to just be a bastard but try to get something done. Or at least that's the way I see it.

I was about to pass the green-and-pink-haired girl in a neon halter and shorts that didn't seem to have an ass when I stopped. "Whose girl are you?"

"You a cop?" That was the reflexive whore response to pretty much anything. But you could tell from her voice that she needed to smoke a lot less.

"No."

She glanced about suspiciously. "Slim Jack," she said, as she looked around wondering where the smack for just saying the name would come from. I started to pull a business card out then remembered I've gotten info from Slim Jack before. He was neither slim, nor was I willing to bet at a big ass Samoan motherfucker like him was born with the name Jack. But his info had always been good and never bitched about the kickback I gave him for it.

"Tell him to give Nick Decker a call. Could be something in it for him." I didn't say anything else but just turned and walked off. I tossed my empty Dr Pepper bottle at the trashcan, missed, and kept walking. It wasn't my job to save the fucking world and somehow it was.

If Uriel had been working at night some of the working girls might have seen. So a pimp might actually know something. I needed intel, so I needed to cast a wide net.

Then it dawned on me who I needed to talk to. Jammer had always referred to it as the Homeless Underground. But Jammer had a way of making things sound better than the reality turned out to be. But bums tended to know places that were safe and places that were dangerous. Places to hunker down in and places to run from. I'd put money on a good bum sniffing out a serial killer before a cop any day of the week. A bum might never thrive, but a good one survived. And survival, a shit ton of the time anyway, was about just noticing things.

I was still miles from the office but that didn't matter right then. I saw a small mom-and-pop Italian restaurant and I turned down the alley behind it. I banged on the door next to the dumpster. I waited and a dishwasher with a damp, stained shirt opened the door with a confused look on his face. Before he could say anything I held up a fifty-dollar bill. I tried to keep a few fifties and a couple hundreds for times I needed answers and didn't feel like talking it out of someone. Right now I needed fast, not cheap, so I was willing to pay for it. I waved the bill between the middle and index finger of my left hand.

"I need three pounds of cheese. I don't care if the shit's turned, I don't care what kind it is, but I fucking need it now." The washer looked at the cash and reached for it. I held it back. "Cheese first, shithead."

He shut the door and I waited a few minutes. I was about to chalk this up as a dry hole when the guy opened the door and held out a brown paper bag with the logo of the restaurant on it. It was a cartoon older lady and chubby husband smiling and holding out a plate of spaghetti. It was cute enough I realized Gretchen and I would be eating here sooner or later; baring the end of the fucking world.

I handed him the cash and opened the bag, there was a block of provolone with mold sprouting at the end and a ziplock bag of shredded parmesan. The bag was at least three pounds if not more. This would do.

You don't go approach royalty without a gift. We lower-class non-royals always needed to bring a tribute, no matter how fucked up or unofficial the royalty was.

I was still miles from the office but that didn't matter. I needed information. I took the bag of cheese and adjusted the carpet-rolled shotgun across my shoulders.

It was time to go see the Rat King.

Chapter Fifteen

The Rat King
"The Sound of Silence" covered by Disturbed

There were a lot of stories about the origin of the Rat King. The one Jammer believed was that he'd been a Ph.D. biologist who worked for some company or another raising rats for experiments. Experiments never really turn out well for rats and having to shovel loads of rats he'd farmed and raised into a furnace after whatever they'd been testing done them in drove him bonkers.

I didn't really care how he came to where he was in life. Window gets a rock thrownthrough it, shattered when a bird slams against it, hot or cold snaps it, or just decides to commit window suicide. All that really matters is that it's fucking broken. What I cared about was what he knew.

The first thing I noticed, which was exactly the first thing I noticed the first time I'd ever come here, was the sound of scratching and scurrying behind the rotting walls.

Now in folklore, a Rat King is in which two rats get their tails stuck together then more and more get tangled up into it until you have a fucked up, undulating ball of rats. Now, I never knew if it was something that could happen in reality or not, but either way, it's jacked up. In the *Teenage Mutant Ninja Turtles,* the Rat King is a rag-wearing, sewer-dwelling villain who controls a swarm of rats. For me, the Rat King was nowhere near as cool as either.

You couldn't look at the guy and not know he had a sad story. Homeless people in general aren't the products of awesome circumstances and decisions, and the Rat King was in a lot of ways worse. He was what I called homeless-fat. No matter what time of year he appeared rotund because of the number of clothes he wore. Layer over layer of dirty, rotting, and fetid fabric wrapped around what I assumed was a crack-skinny frame. His face dropped like it had once had more volume but the air had been let out of the balloon. His hair was thin and wispy and filthy, and whatever color it had once been it was nothing but white now. His eyes were dichromatic, the left one being green and the right one blue. He didn't have a thumb or forefinger on his left hand, and none of the people I'd talked to about him knew how he'd lost it.

Jammer used to take his aid bag and come check on the Rat King every once in a while. Jammer had been a better person than me. But that's how I first met the Rat King.

He was in his nineties, we assumed. He'd mumbled about Normandy; he'd broken into tears mumbling about Bergen-Belsen. The only book he seemed to own was a first edition of the *Diary of Anne Frank.* He'd cry whenever he looked at it.

The shotgun house didn't even have a power line running to it or a meter. The windows were boarded up and the front door lay in the living room. I stepped through the threshold after setting the shotgun bundle on the front porch.

"R.K. It's Nick, Jammer's buddy," I called out into the darkness. I saw the shadow move as the mound of clothes and short human shuffled past a boarded window. I held out the bag of cheese. "I got cheese for you."

I couldn't make out his features in the dark, but the smell hit me like the Macho Man Randy Savage's flying elbow. His thin, gnarled fingers snatched the bag out of my outstretched hand. He opened the top and buried his face in it and I could hear him inhale with the intensity of a guy who had almost drowned but now breached the surface.

"You see a wacky ginger bitch in a red leather jacket?" I asked as his face was still buried in the bag.

"Why?" His voice was tissue paper thin and crinkled.

"Does it matter?" I didn't want to get in a philosophical argument with a probably crazy guy. Philosophers had tried to figure out *why* since the beginning of time. The best answer anyone had ever given, in my opinion, was Lucifer's "Why not?"

"Everybody hurts." He lifted his face from the bag and started shuffling, dropping handfuls of shredded parmesan in the corners.

"Okay, REM." I paused realizing he wasn't going to get the reference. "It's important. Things are going to get fucking worse if I don't find her, R.K."

He looked to me and you could hear the tears as he mumbled, "Anne had such hope..."

"Hemingway said, 'The world is a fine place and worth fighting for.'" I swallowed as he wept. "I'm trying to fight for it, old man. Can you help me out here?"

He looked up, though in the dark I couldn't see the expression on his, what I assumed, was a grime-covered face. "The parks."

I stood there in the silence and saw him reach in the bag and push a handful of cheese into his mouth. From that, I drew the assumption that he wasn't going to say anything beyond that.

"Which park?" Like most cities there were a lot of parks, spanning from big ones you could have festival concerts in and small parks that didn't even cover an acre. Granted saying "the parks" was better than him saying, "in town"...but only barely.

"She's an angel," he muttered around a mouthful of cheese. "I can see it clear. Clear."

Six months ago I would have passed that off as crazy talk. It probably was crazy talk. Just because it's correct doesn't mean it's not batshit insane.

"I know, but she's not aiming for anything good, R.K. Which park?"

"All." He broke off a piece of molded provolone and knelt down. I couldn't see the rat but I could hear the pleased squeak as it started eating from his old, liver-spotted hand. "Every, all, all and every."

"Did she say anything?"

He looked at me and I saw the moonlight glint off his cracked glasses. "She said I was right. Correct. Accurate."

"About what?"

I saw him gesture toward a spot in the shadow. I squinted, and when I couldn't see anything I took out my phone and turned on the flashlight. Setting there, leaning against the wall was a placard that had originally been used for some protest probably, but it'd been painted over by hand and in hand-painted black letters it simply and profoundly proclaimed: THE END IS NIGH.

"Well, that's goddamned comforting, isn't it?" I sighed. "Thanks, R.K."

I turned and stepped back onto the creaking, dry-rotted porch. I breathed deep the fresh air of the street, even though I could still smell and, more disturbing, taste the foul flavor permeating from behind me. I stepped down to the bottom step then sat.

I pulled my phone out then dropped a pin and sent it to Gretchen with the text. "Could use a ride, and an extra-large pizza."

I turned and sat with my back against the wobbly rail and was surprised that it held my weight. A park made sense. They possessed plenty of open ground, wide fields of fire. Fighting in a park seemed a whole lot better than things exploding out into the urban sprawl.

But all that was predicated on it being a normal fight. Uriel was trying to kick off the end of the world. Where it started seemed pretty fucking insignificant considering either way life as we know it on this world would be ending.

I don't know how long I'd sat there but I knew my ass had gone numb by the time she pulled up in the Charger. I managed to get to my feet just in time for her to throw herself in my arms and almost freaking bowl me over.

"Are you okay? Are you hurt? What happened?" she babbled as she squeezed me tight

"I didn't die." I smirked and lifted her off the ground in a hug.

She laughed. "Well, that's obvious."

"How are Yuri and Mary Jo?"

Gretchen smiled as I set her down. "I took them to the office. Mary Jo's sister is coming to get them."

"Good." I paused, thinking back. "Was anyone at the office when y'all got back?"

She shook her head. "No."

"Okay, did you grab the pizza?"

We sat on the trunk of the Charger and both of us took a slice of the extra-large, supposedly New York-style pizza. I folded the slice in half long ways to keep it from flopping too much as I lifted it. We ate quietly and split a Dr Pepper between us. We looked out over the detritus of civilization. This neighborhood was either dead or past saving. The folks who lived there were either lost like the Rat King or there because there was no place else that would take them. The best hope the legitimate people there had was for a developer to come in, buy them out, and wreck the place to put up a combination shopping-area-with-condos above. Maybe they'd make enough to be able to get a start elsewhere.

I could feel eyes on me and Gretchen sitting on the back of a nicer car than had been in that neighborhood for years. Before we'd sat I'd unfurled the carpet roll and now had the sawed-off shotgun propped next to me in the open. That was enough to dissuade any potential negative interest we might gain by being there. Gretchen, God love her, followed suit, and had one of her revolvers sitting out next to her as well.

The pizza wasn't good, but at that time of night, it was *great-considering-the-big-chain-pizzerias-were-closed* great. I got down to the crust when my phone rang. I pulled it out and held it to my ear. "Decker."

"Yo man, heard you wanted to talk." The voice on the other side of the line was oddly nasal for being so low pitched.

"This Slim Jack?" I knew it was Slim Jack, but pimps tended to be vain so proving you knew their name never hurt anything.

"Yeah." His answer was the aggravating combination of annoyed and curious.

"Ask your stable, let me know if any of them have seen a ginger bitch in a red leather jacket hanging around any of the parks. You bring me the good shit that pans out there's a century in it for you." I bit into the crust and chewed as I waited.

There was a good twenty seconds of silence before the deep yet nasally voice replied. "I get back witcha."

The line went dead and I slid the phone back in my suit jacket pocket.

Gretchen glanced at me bemused. "A century? A Benjamin, I get, but a century? Who talks like that anymore?"

I shrugged and crammed the rest of the crust in my mouth. "Dashiell Hammett," I answered around the food.

She laughed and it made me smile even around a mouthful of food.

I hopped off the trunk and closed the pizza box. "You done?"

She nodded and started sucking the grease from her fingers with a deliciously seductive languidly. I knew she knew exactly what she was doing and doing it on purpose, to boot.

I took the box and walked back to the porch and stopped at the door. My eyes couldn't penetrate the shadowy gloom of the shotgun house, but I knew the Rat King was still in there. "Hey, brother," I called into the inky blackness that made a quiet primal part of my brain want to panic. "I got you a pizza. You should eat some of it while it's hot." I held the box out to the full extent of my arms.

A shadow shifted and took the pizza box out of my hands. I dropped them back to my sides and slid them into my pockets.

"What happened to Jammer?" the voice of the Rat King quietly asked from the blackness like a ghost.

"He died." No way around it...and sugar coating has never been my strong suit.

"How?" There was sorrow there, more than you'd expect from someone who had just lost an acquaintance, but less than a father who had lost a son. Who knows how relationships define themselves?

"Like a fucking boss." I couldn't think of a way to explain it better; in a way that would hurt less.

It was quiet for a moment and I turned to walk back to the Charger when I heard the Rat King quietly whisper. "The End is nigh."

"Brother," I muttered as I started down the creaking, rotted steps. "You have no goddamned idea."

Chapter Sixteen

Cruising
"Life is a Highway" Tom Cochran

Gretchen drove the Charger the way I imaged a grandmother would drive a muscle car. She'd turn her blinker on at the beginning of the block she was going to turn from. She accelerated at a pace that made me wonder if the automatic transmission was just idling up. Her turns were slow and wide. The one time a car passed us she eased over until she almost hit the curb.

"You okay?" I asked as I gave my seatbelt a tug. We weren't going fast enough to really need it, but she left me with the impression an accident might be a real possibility.

There wasn't sweat on her forehead but it wouldn't have shocked me if there had been. "I'm fine. Why?"

"I dunno, you interviewing for the job of Miss Daisy's chauffeur?"

Her lips pursed but she didn't take her eyes off the road to glare at me. "NO! Jerk."

"Do you… holy shit. You don't know how to drive do you?" I had to be wrong, I knew I had to be wrong. There was no way that a freaking trained ninja-like Gretchen couldn't know how to drive.

"… Shut up."

"Holy fucking shit!" I laughed.

"I'm sorry, but coming up I learned a lot of stuff but never this, okay?" She sounded a galvanization of annoyed and embarrassed and it was adorable.

"So they didn't teach you to drive at Secret Society Ninja School?" I didn't mean to, but when I said it out loud I ended up laughing even more.

"I'm sorry," she shot back at me. "Do you know the arts of misdirection, stealth, and precision assassination?"

"No." I smirked a big annoying smirk. "But I can drive stick-shift."

We pulled to a stop twenty feet short of the red light. "Hardy har," she mock-laughed.

"You gotta pull up. There's a sensor, and if it doesn't get the car that light's just going to be red forever."

She shot me a dirty look like I was messing with her. But slowly she allowed the car to creep forward closer to the line. She looked even more annoyed when the light went green.

I smile. "For a virgin, you're doing great."

"Shut up. Don't distract me."

"That why you don't have the radio on?"

Her silence spoke volumes.

"Would you rather I drive?" I asked.

"Yes." The hesitation she had given her answer was the same as a teen boy answering *Want Seven Minutes in Heaven with the Playmate of the Year?*

"Well," I thought about it for a minute. "Tough, you're doing fine."

"Bastard." She was starting to smile.

"Naw, they may have turned out to be pieces of shit but they were married."

"Go to hell." You could tell she was mad at herself for not hiding the smile on her lips.

"Sweetie, I'm pretty sure that ticket got bought a long time ago."

At that, she couldn't hold back the laugh she was denying anymore. To her credit, she was keeping the Charger between the lines. Everything she was doing was right, just not necessarily skillful or quick.

"So," I said cautiously, knowing the next thing out of my mouth could probably get me in trouble. "Any of the girls you work with at Sharky's working girls?"

"Working girls?" she asked, coyly curious.

"Yeah, you know."

"I do." She smiled sweetly stopping at the next red light that had caught us. "But I'd rather you have to elaborate."

"Hookers."

She feigned shock and a mock Southern belle accent. "Now, Mr. Decker, why-so-ever would you be looking for a lady of ill repute? That's as shocking as the preacher serving whiskey during communion at a special service." She had pronounced "ever" as *ehv-ah*, said "lady" with at least three As, and "communion" as *ka-mu-union*. She continued in the same accent. "I won't think about it today, I'll think about it tomorrow"—pronounced *to-mah-row* but that was the point I interrupted her.

"Okay, Scarlett O'Hara, enjoying that?"

She grinned. "Immensely."

"Seriously, though, any of the girls from work have a side gig?"

She nodded and, thank God, her voice went back to normal. "A couple, yeah."

"Independent or do they have representation?"

"Representation?" She shot me a sideways glance.

I deserved it for trying to pretty up a dirty thing. "A pimp?"

She shook her head. "No, most of them just get cash for Johns they meet at work."

"That's what I reckoned." I nodded, a bit let down.

"Why?" she asked curiously.

"I put a feeler out on the pimp network about Uriel. I was hoping to cast a wider net."

Gretchen pulled onto Gavin Street, but we were still plenty of blocks from the building. We'd have been there ten minutes ago had I been driving. "Tell me that's not a real name for a thing," she said as she eased through the turn.

"What?"

"The pimp network?" Her eyebrows shot sky-high as she said it.

I shrugged. "I dunno. Sounds official though, doesn't it?"

She smiled. "It really does. Almost like you didn't make it up."

"Well, I didn't make it up," I answered with a defensive smile.

"Bull," she retorted, laughing.

"Jammer made it up," I corrected her.

She nodded. "Okay, that makes sense. So, you've been asking about Uriel on the Pimp Network?"

"Yeah, she's been reconning parks. So, I wanna know if the working girls have noticed anything," I answered with a yawn. I was getting tired.

"That's good thinking," Gretchen admitted, then gave me a smile.

"Well, you don't have to sound so fucking surprised." I laughed.

She laughed. "Sorry."

"My shit always works sometimes." I stuck my tongue out.

Gretchen stopped the car and looked at me with her jaw almost on her chest. "That's why you got the Mike Lowery Ferrari!"

"Huh?"

She'd just tossed a curveball and instead of me swinging at it, it'd beaned me.

"'My shit always works sometimes'. That's literally a Will Smith line from *Bad Boys*—verbatim."

I thought about it for a second. "Yeah, but in *Bad Boys* he drove a Porsche. He didn't get the Ferrari until *Bad Boys II*."

She bit the corner of her lip. "That's true." She slowly got the car going again.

"The thing I've been chewing on," I said chuckling as I watched her extreme concentration, "is if Gabrielle was going to give me a Ferrari, why the *Bad Boys II* Ferrari and not *Robin One*?"

"You know," she admitted, "on the surface, *Robin One* makes more sense, but I get why she didn't." We stopped at a yellow light that a more experienced driver would have ran. "You can't grow the mustache."

I shot her a wounded and dirty look. "I can grow a damned mustache."

She smiled consolingly. "Yes, you can grow a 'stache, but not the Selleck Stache."

I gave it a ponder for a moment. "That guy is fucking blessed by the gods of righteous facial hair."

"Yep, the other thing is you wear suits all the time. Magnum never wore a suit unless he had to for a gig." She gestured at my tieless suit and Chucks. "This is just a life choice you've made."

"Hey!" I glanced at myself. The Armani suits Lucifer had hooked me up with were far superior to the cheap things I'd worn when I'd first met Gretchen. "A man has to have standards."

"Some men have standards." She batted her lashes at me. "You have a uniform."

I laughed because not laughing would have hurt. The truth hurts. Bullets hurt worse, but that was kind of an apples-to-oranges scenario.

We got back to the office and it took twelve minutes and forty-one seconds for Gretchen to park the Charger—not that I timed it or anything. I totally timed it. But she managed to get the muscle car into the spot without hitting the Ferrari.

We took the stairs up and saw the office lights on through the powdered glass door. I opened the door with the sawed-off double-barrel in my right hand. The look in Mary Jo's eyes was frightened but controlled. Yuri looked like he was spoiling for a fight; my hope was it was with someone other than me. Even with the Wrath of God, I was pretty sure that Russian bastard could take me.

I saw Yuri's eyes dart to the boomstick, so I asked with confident nonchalance. "So, what do I owe ya for this?" I jiggled it with my hand to draw attention to it.

Yuri stomped to me with an angry intensity and then wrapped his arms around me pulling me into a bear hug. Mary Jo, not wanting to be left out, grabbed Gretchen. They squeezed each of us, and then they switched. After, there was a flurry of conversation that broke down into one statement and five questions. *We called the cops. Who was that? What the hell is going on? How the hell did you survive that? What do you need us to do?* And lastly, and also my favorite, *the fuck?*

For an instant, I turned into Inigo Montoya. "Let me explain. No, we don't have time. Let me sum up." I went on to give them the short and skinny on the situation. World was ending, probably. As fucked up as it was, Yuri didn't really question it, God love that Russian bastard.

Mary Jo sat in one of the office chairs with her jaw dropped like she was doing a nutcracker impression. Yuri just nodded and when I was through asked the question proving what kind of grand bastard he was at his core. "I can get Draganov. When you need Yuri?"

I couldn't help but smile. I saw Gretchen wipe the corner of her eyes but obviously, she wasn't crying...well, then again, she was definitely crying.

"I'll let you know when I need it, Yuri."

I poured drinks and we finished them just about the time Mary Jo's phone dinged with a text. The Uber she sent for was there, and her sister was expecting them.

At the door Yuri held out Jammer's Kimber 1911.

"You keep it, Yuri, just to be safe," I assured him with a wave of my hand.

He adamantly shook the pistol then opened his jacket revealing a brace of Makarov pistols. "Yuri safe."

I took Jammer's pistol then shifted it to my left hand so Yuri and I could shake. Mary Jo and Gretchen hugged again. They left without another word, because really what was there to say? I shut the door after they'd headed down the stairwell. Then I wrapped my arms around Gretchen and held her there for a moment.

"What now?" she asked quietly into my suit jacket.

I glanced out the window and could see the horizon getting lighter; it'd be daylight soon enough.

"Let's try to get some sleep. See if shit gets clearer after we get some rest."

She nodded and we headed back.

It felt like my socks peeled off my feet instead of pulled. I got my shirt off and accepted that my Old Spice deodorant needed a new liberal application, but I said *fuck it* and would try to remember when I put a shirt back on. I hung my underarm rig off the corner of the headboard and put my 1911 under the pillow as I slid into bed. The sheets were deliciously cool and Gretchen was warm. It felt so good spooning up behind her it had to be wrong, because right never felt that good.

I shut my eyes and instantly drifted off. It was the bliss brought on by exhaustion or would have been had it not been for the knocking on the goddamned outer office door.

"Not it," Gretchen whispered, and I didn't have to look to tell she had her finger pressed to the tip of her nose.

I rolled away from her and kicked my legs off the bed. I looked at the clock and realized I'd been in bed for a total of four minutes. I pulled on my pants and tugged a T-shirt over my head as I stumbled toward the door, 1911 gripped reflexively in my dick-beater. I yawned as I stepped into the outer office. I could see the silhouette of a person banging on the wood door as opposed to the door's powdered glass window. There was a courtesy to that.

I banged my knee on the corner of Agnes's desk and hopped on one foot to the door where I unlocked it. I thumbed back the hammer of my pistol, holding it behind my thigh, and pulled the door open.

There stood Switch, in a blue hospital gown with yellow ducks, and with an annoyed look on his face. "The hell, man?"

Chapter Seventeen

"The Hell, Man?"
"The Boys Are Back in Town" Thin Lizzy

I don't think it would shock anyone to hear that I asked literally the first thing that popped in my head: "What the fuck are you wearing?"

Switch was an early- to mid-fifties subcontinental guy with plenty of gray in his righteous beard. But he stood there in a light blue long shirt-looking thing with off-red roses on it. He had red socks on his feet with yellow grippy paws coming up the sides, so I assumed they covered the bottom.

My second thought was I wanted a pair of those socks because the tile floor of the office was cold and when I got up in the middle of the night to use the can I constantly had to remind myself that I was too much a traditional man for slippers. Those socks would be perfect.

"I just got out of the hospital." He turned and made it painfully obvious that that wasn't a long shirt he was wearing a barely tied hospital gown.

"Well, fuck, man, come on in." I stood to the side and held the door. From the back I heard Gretchen stirring. Either we'd woken her up or she'd not fallen asleep either. "Do you want some other clothes or anything?"

"A drink." He was adamant about that. "You're taller and skinnier than me. None of your shit is gonna fit."

I pulled the Macallan out of the drawer and splashed some into a glass that I hadn't cleaned from earlier, but there wasn't lipstick on it so I handed it to Switch. He took it and slammed it back like Jäger at a frat party.

Gretchen ran out of the back in shorts and a T-shirt and hugged herself into Switch's side. "It's so good to see you."

He smiled at her. "Well, you and Megatron have been visiting." He pointed an accusatory finger at me. "But that son of a bitch never visited once."

I almost corrected him *son of a demon,* but son of a bitch was probably just as accurate, depending on what metric you were measuring with.

"Hey," I knew it was probably pointless to defend myself, but Mickey would always tell Rocky to keep his mitts up. "I fucking hate it when I'm laid up and people pop around. If I'm laid out I'd RATHER be left the fuck alone. Do unto others, cock bag."

Switch set the glass down and Gretchen extricated herself from the grasp she had held him. "You could have snuck me a fucking burger." Switch still sounded surly, but he didn't argue my point so I took that as a little victory.

"What if I had a box of some of Jammer's shit? Would you wear any of that?"

Switch helped himself to another splash of Scotch and I went in the back, coming back with a printer paper box with the word "Jammer" scrawled across the side in black marker and an inarticulate hand. I set it on Agnes's desk and Switch flipped the top off and started rummaging through its contents. He came up with a pair of olive drab cargo pants that were cut off into frayed knee-length shorts. He bent and started tugging them up his legs right there in the office, but luckily at the angle we were standing, Gretchen and I were spared a shocking view by the gown, box, and desk combined. He then pulled off the gown and pulled on the black *Han Shot First* T-shirt that was iconic Jammer.

"I think some shoes are in there," Gretchen offered helpfully.

Switch shook his head. "Do I want the crazy foot funk that Jammer, flat-footed bastard that he was, had? No, thanks." Yet there was a pain in his voice. Switch missed Jammer almost as much as I did. "Plus, there's a pair of good boots in my truck." He paused. "Where is my truck?"

"We put it in storage," Gretchen assured him. "We even made sure the storage place got paid, too. That way your truck didn't end up on *Storage Wars*, or some knock-off thereof."

Switch paused and shot a wary glance at Gretchen. "Did you really just say 'thereof?'"

She nodded enthusiastically.

"What the hell?" Switch sighed.

"What?" My lips turned up into what I knew was an annoying smile. "Just because her lexicon ranges beyond the pale of the common vernacular isn't a sin worthy of chastisement or further derision."

Gretchen beamed; Switch chuckled and shook his head. "You can go to hell, Decker."

I shrugged. "Sooner or later."

"So what's the plan?" Switch asked as he plopped in Agnes's seat.

"Well, first," I asked, "how the fuck did you get out of the hospital? Last I checked you were laid up with fuck-all wrong with you."

He scratched his beard. "I'll be honest, I don't know. One second I was lying there, the next I felt fine. All the IV catheters were out and, I mean, you can't even tell where they were."

"Like you re-spawned in a video game?" Gretchen asked with an insane glee in her eyes as she leaned her elbows on the desk.

Switch and I glanced at her. "Okay," I said cautiously. "That's the winner of the Nerdiest Thing You've Ever Said Award."

Switch nodded in agreement. "That made me want to break your glasses and take your lunch money."

"I don't wear glasses," Gretchen reassured us. That made me picture her wearing glasses. Imagining a sexy librarian look. That worked. There was a quasi-long pause, then she asked, "You're picturing me wearing glasses, aren't you?"

"Yes," I said honestly. Switch shrugged.

"And?" she asked coyly.

I shrugged. "I wouldn't kick ya outta bed for eating crackers."

Switch nodded.

Gretchen laughed.

"Well," I said putting the Macallan bottle back in the drawer—I knew if I didn't we'd end up getting drunk and I had a feeling in the back of my mind that being sloshed wouldn't help things later in the day. I've not learned a lot in life, but I'd learned to trust my gut..."looks like Gabrielle kept her end of shit."

Switch looked confused.

Gretchen calmly and with a far more rational tone that I think any of our lives deserved explained, "Nick did a job for the archangel Gabrielle and the deal was she got you fixed up." She then turned her shining eyes to me. "Want to give him his present?"

Switch glanced at us suspiciously at that. But I got up and went to the back, coming back with a case larger than a lunch box but smaller than a briefcase. He slowly opened it like he expected to get glitter bombed; I couldn't blame him for it because the second I'd thought of it I'd wished I'd done it.

Inside the case lay a Glock 19 Gen 3; it had been on sale. Modified with a lighter trigger, a flared mag well, and tritium night sights. Next to the 19 was a Glock 43, single-stack subcompact pistol. Both had two magazines and Kydex holsters for all; the 19 on his hip and the 43 in an ankle rig.

"We tossed your Glock 17 in the river after the shootout because, you know, it'd been in a shoot out," Gretchen explained as Switch pulled back the slide on the 19. "But we owed ya, so Merry Christmas, Happy Chauncha, Groovy Kwanza, Happy No Special Day Because You're Jehovah's Witness."

She probably would have gone on, but Switch laughed. "Thanks." He held the Glock 19 up to his ear after dropping the mag, then making sure nothing was under the hammer and pulled the trigger, dry firing it. "How light is that trigger?"

"It's a Glock Ghost three-point-five-pound trigger," I told him.

Switch nodded. "Did you do the trigger work and the rest of the mods?"

I laughed. "Would you trust it if I did?"

"No." He pulled back the slide, inserted a mag, dropped the slide and slid the pistol into the Kydex holster, which he began to thread onto the belt he took from Jammer's box.

Gretchen smiled reassuringly. "Then it's good we got Yuri to do it."

Switch attached the ankle holster around his ankle and wiggled the toes of his sock-clad feet. He looked ridiculous in the outfit and armed like that, but I felt better seeing him armed after him being laid up in the hospital for so long.

I reminded myself next time Gabrielle popped up, no matter how ill-timed or annoying, I needed to thank her.

"So," Switch slowly asked, "what is the plan?"

"Well," Gretchen offered, "the world is ending."

"Metaphorically or literally?"

"Literally," she assured him.

"Literally as in *entropy and the eventual energy death of the universe* or literally as in tomorrow?" One of the great things about Switch was how he just rolled with things while still hoping for the best.

"Tomorrow at the latest." Her smile didn't make that less daunting of a prospect.

"So, what's the plan?"

"Try to stop it," I said with all the confidence I didn't feel.

"Okay, what's the first step?" Switch could be a persistent bastard.

"Us getting dressed, I guess, then getting you shoes," I offered with a shrug.

He mock-laughed. "Ha Hardy Har."

"No, seriously, chill here for a minute," I said as Gretchen and I hopped up. We went to the back and took a quick shower without making a game of it. We dried, again, without any play, and then began getting dressed. I pulled on a black suit and my Chucks, my underarm rig under my jacket. Gretchen pulled on a gray tank top, black short shorts, her pouch belt, and holstered her pistols behind her back under her jacket, which would have been a duster had it passed her knees.

Switch was waiting in the office trying to get onto Agnes's desktop computer but was having trouble negotiating the password. He might as well have been trying to navigate the Northwest Passage as opposed to figuring out the password of the detail-oriented efficiency machine I had as a secretary. "What's the password?"

"I dunno. It's Agnes's, not mine."

"Isn't she your secretary?" He pushed the keyboard away like it was a plate of *escargot*.

"More or less."

"Then shouldn't you know how to get into all the electronics in your office? Including her desktop?" His tone reminded me of a genetics professor dealing with a creationist student.

"You'd think that, but then again some people still dig disco," I countered with a smile.

"Well, now you're dressed," he observed. "Gretchen, you did way better than Nick at that."

"Thank you." She beamed at the backhanded compliment. I mean, it has never been difficult to dress better than me.

"So, now, what's the plan?" Switch asked pointedly at me.

"Uriel, another goddamned archangel, has been reconning parks. I think it's doing battle-map analysis and shit like that." It sounded strange, sounding like I knew what I was talking about.

"Okay?" His words implied a statement, but his tone offered a question so that's how I took it. "So, we need to figure out which park?" he asked as he stood, already ready to roll. Apparently, spending six months in a hospital bed left some people restless.

I nodded.

"Breakfast first though, right?" Gretchen asked with the implied and easily heard need for coffee.

"Most important meal of the day," Switch agreed.

I sighed. "Fucking fine." I wanted to go back to bed, actually to bed really. But that's life, as the Stones eloquently explained it in the classic *You Can't Always Get What You Want*.

Then we all glanced over as there was a knock on the office door.

"Jesus Christ," I muttered, "what's the fucking point of having posted office hours if no one's going to fucking pay attention to them?"

I walked over to the door and took a deep breath and fixing my best fake smile to my lips as I pulled the door open.

Then a swarm of flies exploded in my face.

Chapter Eighteen

Lord of the Fucking Flies
"Almost Easy" Avenged Sevenfold

Now when I said I was hit in the face with flies, I don't mean ten or so flies buzzed into my face. I mean a goddamned firehouse gushed in my face, but instead of water it was fucking flies. The world went dark and it sounded like an old TV had exploded with static. The blast of flies was enough to knock me back onto my ass, which was a good thing as it forced me out of the fly stream. That wasn't to say my face wasn't covered in flies.

It felt like a sucker punch, and that pissed me off on two levels. First, it offended the Teddy Roosevelt part of my brain that respected a fair fight. Now, I'll fight dirty. I'll shoot first and into a back, but still. Secondly, it reminded me of a movie, though visually impressive, the concepts of character and story were completely lost on the director. I felt the Wrath, and I let it fly.

My head erupted in flame, wreathing my skull and burning all the flies to tiny cinders. I couldn't see, but I imagined it to resemble a Greek Hoplite helmet. Then the fire coursed quickly down my right arm and the xiphos of fire grew in my hand.

On my back, I saw him in the hallway. To say he was fat would be a gross (mind the pun) understatement. His shape was vaguely human but in a rotund cartoonish way. He had five rolls of neck that flowed into his shoulders like a zigarut. His round arms had long flaps of skin like he could use them to fly away if he wasn't too lazy to flap his damn arms. You couldn't see his feet because of hyperbolic cankles. He looked naked, but if he had any clothes, or sex for that matter, they were hidden under rolls of flesh. His eyes were a sickly puss-like yellow. His teeth were dead and rotting.

Fugly didn't cover it.

I kicked my legs and rolled up into a crouch as he—I assumed he, praying that no female would ever be that unfortunate—opened that rotted mouth and screamed in a teeth-grinding falsetto. Another stream of flies shot from ugly suck. Near instantly the Sword dissipated from my right hand, the flame ran up my arm over my shoulders and down my left arm as I brought it before me. The shield of fire formed as the fly stream impacted into it. I didn't even feel the impact; apparently, the Wrath of God was as good as vibranium. The flies burned off on the shield and its concentric circles of fire with a star in the middle. The falsetto stopped and the fly stream stopped with it.

The flame moved back up my arm, across my shoulders, and down my right emerging again as the xiphos in my hand. I kicked my legs like pistons and started sprinting for him. Weapons appeared in his hands; whether they appeared there or if he'd been hiding them in fat I'll never know. In his left was a fleshy looking hammer that resembled a large, eight-inch-by-eight-inch meat hammer. In his right hand was a wicked-looking cleaver that appeared to be made of bone.

Now, when I'd fought Zadkiel and Baalberieth I hadn't known what I was doing, so I let the Wrath guide me and just went with it. In the past six months, Gretchen had been training me in all her Martial Arts *Kung Fu* ninja glory. What I'd learned is my basic fighting style is still nineteenth-century Irish boxing, and in regards to sword fighting I just needed to roll with the Wrath.

In the confines of the hallway, I knew he wouldn't be able to get good swings in and would be reliant on thrusts. The short-bladed fire xiphos in my hand was built for that kind of work. Neither of his weapons were designed for that kind of work. It felt weird, actually having an advantage. It made me paranoid.

He thrust with the bone hammer. I stepped inside it and thrust with the xiphos but he managed to get the cleaver in the way. I grabbed the wrist of his cleaver hand and yanked. I instantly wished I'd hadn't. You could feel the crawling under his waxy pulpy skin. But my yank did pull his fat ass off balance and I gave a short slash with the Fiery Sword, biting deep into his cankle. The sword left a long, ragged tear. Immediately maggots and puss began spilling from the wound and flowing onto the tile floor. It smelled like the fetid armpit of a three-day-old corpse left rotting in a pile of Limburger cheese.

I dove and bounced off the wall. I came up to face three unhappy surprises. First, the fly spitting shit head wasn't alone. There were four imps, for lack of a better term. They were all about four feet tall, horns, goat legs, work shirts like you imagine a mechanic wearing, and long knives. They made me think of if a group of Fawns left Narnia and had spent the last four years working as slot machine repairmen in Tunica, Mississippi.

The second surprise was not that I was between the fat fuck and these bags of ass; none of who had a look on their faces that seemed pleasant.

The last surprise: Megatron had poked her head out of her door. Her face was a mix of confusion and fear even under all that goddamned caked-on *geisha* makeup.

"Shut the fucking door!" I yelled as I started running toward the imps. I wanted to finish the fat fucker because he seemed more of a threat than the imps, but at least one of them had turned their attention to Megatron. As annoying as she was, she was one of us. The first imp I came to swung his knife. I blocked his wrist with my left forearm and thrust into his gut with the Fiery Sword hard enough to lift him off the ground high enough that the tip of the blade poked out of his back and stabbed into the ceiling's acoustic tile.

I half-turned and slung my arm, hurling the impaled imp toward the fat fucker like a *jai alai* ball. As the imp tumbled through the air I watched as a gash appeared in the fat fucker's shoulder as Gretchen stabbed through a great flap of fat with the Spear. The wound she left gushed maggots and puss, but it also smoldered like burning peat.

I whipped my head around in time to see one of the imps lunging with his knife. I grabbed his wrist with my left hand; it was fucking hot. I twisted it and kicked him between his goat legs. There was so much fur down there I wasn't sure I hit anything but the way he doubled over felt gratifying.

The third tried lunging in over the body of his comrade on the ground. I grabbed him by his shirt while he was in the air and slammed him head-first into the wall. The plaster in the wall cracked and fell in large shards, but more importantly, the imp's head bent backward on his neck like a fucking Pez dispenser.

The fourth imp looked wide-eyed and started to run. That made me even madder. I sprinted and grabbed him by one of his horns and jerked his head back ramming the Fiery Sword into his back and out his chest. He didn't cry out; there was no explosion of energy or gush of blood. He simply went limp as I let go of his horn. His corpse fell to the floor as it slid off the burning blade.

I heard the gunfire behind me and turned, watching Gretchen ducked to the left side of the hall as Switch emptied the Glock 19 magazine into the fat fucking demon. I was convinced these asshats were demons; it was too obvious. The problem was that demons could take a bullet just as easy as an angel—or archangel, anyway.

Before Switch's empty magazine hit the ground Gretchen was back in there with a dancer's grace. The fat fucker brought the fleshy hammer down and she easily side-stepped it and twirled the Spear around. The tip bit into his wrist slicing at least four inches deep and four inches long. He brought the cleaver high, and she ducked and twisted while ramming the Spear tip through the corpulent fat of the left cankle.

I heard the scream and watched Switch duck back behind the door frame as the stream of flies shot past where he'd just been. Gretchen was at an angle where she could see me. She dove trying to get around the fat fucker the same way I had, but he was onto that game. He turned and jumped, crushing her between his fat and the wall. I started sprinting toward him.

The imp I'd kicked in the possible nuts was pulling himself to his hands and hooves. I kicked him in the fucking gourd without even breaking my stride. I roared and his yellow eyes went wide with fear as he saw me coming full tilt.

He pulled back off the wall and Gretchen fell to the floor with a gasp. He screamed and shot the gush of flies at me. I grabbed the Sword with both hands and held it in front of me. The burning blade split the stream of flies and fired them to each side of me as I closed.

I didn't stab or slash or do anything articulate with the blade. I jumped and grabbed one of the waxy flabs of fat dangling from his neck and gripped it tight enough I could feel my fingers through the adipose. My knees rammed my momentum into his chest, sending him back. I felt his knees starting to give way. Using the fat handhold to steady me as he fell backward, that was when I slashed with the Sword.

I swung and hacked again and again. I was lost in a red haze. The fiery blade biting through corpulent flesh and the tile floor all the same. Puss and maggots sprayed along the tile and onto the wall. I let go of his neck fat and gouged my fingers into his yellow eyes and kept hacking. Puss flowed around my fingers.

I was so lost in the fury I didn't even notice his head had come off and I was holding it in my left hand like a bowling ball till I felt her arms. She slipped them around me, just under my arms and her cheek rested against the back of my neck. I could feel her breath on the back of my right ear.

"It's okay," she whispered. The Sword evaporated from my hand.

After fighting Uriel I'd hacked up at least ten cars on that road with the Sword before coming across an old Datsun pickup. My first vehicle had been an old Datsun pickup. I loved that piece of shit so much that it had been enough to loosen the Wrath's grip on me enough to let go of the Sword. It was always easier to do with Gretchen.

Switch patted my other shoulder as he moved past us and down the hall.

I turned my head and asked quietly into the top of her head, "You okay?" I dropped the severed head and shook my hand a little, trying to flick off some of the puss.

She nodded. "I need a shower, though."

I chuckled. "That fat fuck was greasy, wasn't he?"

"Like an extra meat, extra cheese pizza," she agreed with a light laugh.

"What the fuck was that?" I asked no one in particular.

I turned my head when I heard the door of the stairwell open. I saw Agnes step out. She surveyed the scene and her face held a fairly adorable and endearing mix of confusion and resignation. She stepped past Switch and then hopped over the mess of maggots and puss, an impressive feat in her four-inch heels. She stopped at the office door and looked at the mess of flies buzzing around. She sighed. "I'll get the flypaper out." She disappeared into the office but left the door open for us.

Gretchen laughed at that then slid in under my left arm. I looked down at the severed head and nudged it with my foot. "What in the holy goddamned fuck was that?"

"I don't know," she quietly confessed.

"Why don't we ask this little guy?" Switch asked.

We turned and saw him standing there, holding the last surviving imp by his horn. He'd zip-tied the imp's hands together in front of him. The imp was bleeding from a cut along the right side of his face where I'd kicked him in the freaking head.

Switch smiled. "Want some answers?"

I nodded. "Let's make this little cock bag sing like Luciano fucking Pavarotti."

Chapter Nineteen

How Do You Interrogate A Freaking Demon?
"Keep Your Hands To Yourself" Georgia Satellites

S o we used zip-ties to basically hogtie the little imp bitch demon. Then we'd thrown him in the trunk of Gretchen's Charger and drove out to the place Jammer had set up six months before, where we had planned on interrogating Doc Douchebag. The demon didn't say anything, just grunted a bunch of pig-like squeals. I duct-taped the imp to a chair while Switch and Gretchen ran out for "supplies," though what kind of supplies you get for a demon interrogation was beyond me.

The bastard's beady little black eyes just stared. Not *horror movie creep you out* stared, but more just, *annoyed the fuck out of you* stared.

"You really want to make this shit easy you could start talking before they get back." I leaned back in my chair; it was identical to his except I wasn't taped to it. "Fuck all knows what they're going to bring to torture you with. If I'm honest this is a little outside our wheelhouse." I smiled. "But goddamned if we're not quick learners and energetic participants."

"You're talking too much." His voice was half-squeal, half-falsetto. It was what you'd imagine a pig would sound like if you kicked it in the nuts and it could talk.

"Then lighten the mood with some pleasant and informative conversation." I crossed my arms as I leaned back.

It stared dead-eyed at me. "What would you like to know?"

"Lets start easy: what's your name?"

"You couldn't pronounce my name." He actually snorted before answering.

"What should I call ya then?" I remembered Bruce Campbell— guardian angel's real name wasn't Bruce Campbell—so I figured the imp bitch was shooting me straight on that.

"Murdock."

"What were your buddies' names?" I figured if I could get him talking he might spill some shit he didn't realize was important.

"The boss was Beelzebub."

I raised an eyebrow. "So, boss, not buddy, huh? Strictly professional with that one?"

He nodded.

"And the other three?" I leaned up resting my elbows on my knees.

"Hannibal, B.A. and Face," he answered with all seriousness.

"Bullshit." My answer was unthought and instinctually reflexive.

He shrugged as much as you can duct-taped to a chair.

"You are fucking telling me," I said slowly, making sure I didn't make this sound more stupid than it already was, "that I took down the, I dunno, demonic A-Team?"

Again, and it was getting annoying, he shrugged.

"Where's the cool van?" I asked, half-curious, half-playing along.

"Haha." His mock laugh was so mocking it was drier than the Namib Desert.

"So why the A-Team?" I didn't care for the apparent fact that the most formative live-action TV show had been co-opted by demons, and runty looking ones at that.

"Name me another easily remembered foursome," he sardonically offered.

"The Beatles, Channel 4 News Crew, the Ghostbusters, the Four Musketeers…"

"Three Musketeers," he interrupted.

"No, you started with three. Athos, Porthos, and Aramis. But they got joined by Dartanion, didn't they? Asshole."

He cocked his head sideways at a wholly unnatural angle. "What's the name of the book?"

"*The Three Musketeers.*"

"And what's the name of the movie?" He rolled his head to the same angle but the other way.

"Which one?"

"Michael York, Oliver Reed, Richard Chamberlain, Raquel Welch, Charlton Heston, and Christopher Lee." He licked his upper lip and I noticed his tongue was forked with a cartoonish absurdity. "You know, the good version."

"*The Three Musketeers*, but there was *The Four Musketeers.*" The the little bitch demon think he was going to out-movie-trivia me?

"And the Kiefer Sutherland, Charlie Sheen, Oliver Platt, Chris O'Donnell version by Disney that Tim Curry couldn't quite make live up to its predecessor?"

I sighed. "*The Three Musketeers.*"

"Want me to keep going?" He asked in a manner so off-handed it belayed the fact it was duct-taped to a chair.

"I want you to shut the fuck up unless you plan on giving me what I need without me having to resort to what we both know is coming if you keep this up." I felt the Wrath bubbling in me. Maybe it was the lack of sleep, or the recent fight, or just the time and proximity to the demon. I didn't know, and I honestly didn't care right then and there.

"You haven't asked a substantial question yet." He spoke slowly with what sounded like an *oink* for punctuation.

I looked into his beady demon eyes. "What the fuck were you after at my office?"

"The Sword." It was an easy answer to give but the little bastard gave it pretty bluntly.

"What about Lucifer?" I asked quietly. I knew Uncle Lew didn't want the Sword, he wanted balance.

"What about him?" He was trying to be a Gretchen-level of coy and failing miserably.

"Don't toy with me, cock bag." I felt the Wrath trying to bubble up in my gut.

He smiled. "Beelzebub wasn't exactly following the party line."

"And why's that?"

The imp tried to shrug. "Who says Heaven has to win?"

I smirked and leaned back and crossed my arms. "Well, seems they got numbers, quality, and you know... The capital-F Father on their side."

"The last Throne sanction was Sodom and Gamora. Since then, what's he done since then besides the 2004 World Series."

"What about the plagues of Egypt?" I arched my eyebrows, trying to antagonize him into talking more.

"That was our first try and jackasses didn't give credit where credit was due."

"Huh?"

The imp sighed. "So the Father, through Gabrielle anyway, sure did go tell Moses to free his people. But that's it." He smiled, and it seemed to legitimately be pleasure-filled. "But water to blood, frogs, lice, flies, livestock plague, boils, hail and fire, locusts, three days of darknesss..." He smiled like he was removing the most succulent dish he ever tasted. "Murder of the firstborn." He leaned in as much as he could, strapped to the chair. "Do those sound like the acts of your omnibenevolent, omnipotent, and omnipresent Father?"

"As opposed to what?"

He licked his lips with that forked tongue with a wet sucking sound. "A bunch of demons trying to help His People get home because they want to as well..."

"Bullshit."

"Some of us wanted to go home. You think Hell belongs to us? It's OUR prison. Doesn't make it any better to be the spiritual overflow for you meat bags who don't make the divine cut. But when the door slams we're trapped forever." He sounded almost plaintiff like. "We wanted to go home so we tried to help Moses on the mission given him by the Father because we wanted to go home."

"Bullshit."

He sighed. "Sorry, I forgot who I was talking to. Mister *Found Family*, Mister *Walked Away From Home and Never Looked Back*, Mister *Sociopath Doesn't Give a Shit*, Mister *Wanna be My-Life-Moves-In-One-Direction-Don-Freaking-Forward-Draper*. News flash, meat bag, some people wish they could go home. Some people long for it. Some of us, as the phrase goes, would give our left nut to go back home. To be welcomed with the open arms the Father offers you rotting bags of flesh." A literal tear rolled from his eye. "You meat bags get to go... and I—we—never get to go back. Go home."

I chewed on it a second. Mainly because it hadn't dawned on me how much pretty much any demon in Hell probably knew about me. One shape form or fashion all of them would have known my mom. All of them would have gotten the boot the same as her back in the beginning. Maybe because I'm just the fucked-up guy I am because deep down I'm just an unwitting celebrity kid.

Then the idea quickly evaporated. I became the asshole I chose to be. Not because fate or the genetic fucking lottery. Fuck that little imp motherfucker.

"Boo fucking hoo." I leaned in on my elbows. "I got permanently banned from a Walmart, want to know why? Because of something I did—that ban's on me."

That tear lingered at his cheek just at the corner of his mouth. "How do you get banned from a Walmart?"

"Doesn't fucking matter. Lucifer himself said your side can't win. So why make a play for the Sword?"

"You didn't know she was alive when you took down the Heaven's Hotdogs. You didn't know you'd win when you fought the Bearer. You did it because you hoped."

"So you're telling me hope's a hell of a drug?"

He nodded.

I sighed. "There anything useful you can tell me?"

"Not that I'm willing to," he said with an odd resignation. Like he knew what was coming, what had always been coming since the moment we strapped him to the chair, the moment he showed up in my hall, the moment he was created.

"Torturing you wouldn't do a goddamned bit of good, would it?"

He shook his head.

I sighed and got up. I walked around behind him and he didn't turn his head to watch. I grabbed him by the horns and started twisting. I wrenched his head around a full three-hundred-and-sixty degrees, then another one-eighty. Giving him a full five hundred and forty degrees of rotation. His chin sat between his diminutive shoulder blades. I let go of the horns and stepped back.

He looked up. "Did you really expect that to work? I mean, you've seen Linda Blair in *The Exorcist*, right?"

"Are you going to vomit pea soup all over me?" I asked, suddenly concerned about my black suit. I didn't want to have to change clothes again today.

"Would it help you finish this?" He cocked his head and it looked jacked up doing that backward.

Curiosity hit me like a Mack truck. "Why do you want it?"

"Want what?" His tongue snaked out and dragged along that tear stain.

"To kill you." I stuffed my hands in my pockets like I was looking for something but I knew I'd never find the answers I needed there. "What happens to a demon or an angel when they die?"

"Nothing." It was said flat and emotionless as the word itself.

"So, there's no real ramification?" That seemed like a letdown.

"No," he smiled wistfully. "You meat bags get Heaven or Hell. Us...we cease to be. Oblivion."

"Why would you want that?" Even shitty existence seemed better than the alternative of *None*.

"Because it's better than Hell, and once Armageddon kicks off that's all we're going to have left if we lose." For the first time, I heard a tinge of panic behind Murdock's voice.

"So Oblivion is the lesser evil?" That was a shitty realization to have dawn on you.

He nodded.

I walked over and started unrolling the duct tape around his arms. I could have cut it off his wrists, but that would have been quicker and less painful and I didn't see any reason to give any courtesy to the imp.

"What are you doing?" he asked as I got one wrist free.

"I'm letting you go." It seemed obvious, but apparently he needed it said.

"Why?" If confusion were coins that imp bastard would have been rich.

"Because the alternative is giving you what you want, and frankly I don't think you've earned it, and it ain't my job to give it to you."

"How do you know I won't try to kill you?" He stayed in the chair but rubbed his wrists.

I shrugged. "I don't, but I don't really care. The world's ending, right?"

He slowly hopped up and stepped toward the door. He paused and looked back. "Just after sunset tonight, at least that's what Beelzebub thought."

I nodded. "See ya then, Murdock." He stepped out and was gone. I pulled out my phone and called Gretchen. "Hey, yeah, we're done here so don't worry about the stuff. Where do you want to meet?"

I looked at the clock on my phone: 0934.

Abandon All Hope

We had about nine hours to save the world and not a damn clue how to do it.

Chapter Twenty

Astra-Mugs: Where Dreamers Come To Fuel
"Creep" originally by Radiohead but preformed by Vega Choir

H ad I had my way we'd have gone to Waffle House.

I hate coffee shops. I know *hate* is a strong word, but it seems more polite than *fucking loath from the depths of my very soul.* Oddly the places themselves are fine, most of the time. Coffee shops as locations are places that I wouldn't say I felt fine about, but as locations, they didn't make me feel anything. Where was I in my life that sociopathic ambivalence as preferable to any feeling?

So maybe the more acceptable statement wouldn't be *I hate coffee shops* but *I hate coffee shop P-fucking-eople.* Coffee shop people shared the trait I hated most in fringe political assholes, creative douches, evangelical pricks, and your average parent: they were vocal about things. I don't care what your definition of "free speech," your thoughts on GITMO, gun control, abortion, or Article

One Section Seven of the Constitution happen to be. I don't give a shit about your Zine. I'm literally the nephew of Lucifer so go peddle the wares of your gospel shop somewhere else. No honest person cares that your kid's special according to his underfunded and over-worked teachers, who really want you to shut the fuck up and get out of their office. The older I get the more I find common cause with my Old Man in his struggle throughout my childhood: for things to just be quiet. Coffee shops are like magnets for assholes who lack the ability to shut the fuck up and keep it to themselves.

I was already tired. Thus the fact I found myself sitting at a small round table in *Astra-Mugs: Where Dreams Come To Fuel* did absolutely zilch to improve my mood. Everything about the place seemed specifically designed to piss me off and make the Fiery Sword unleash from me and start the burning of the world right there and then. The walls were covered in a nonsensical mismatch of "art" by local artists who, by dint of talent and Adam Smith's "invisible hand," would forever be struggling. There was a framed print out of an article from the internet about the overdose and death of Shannon Moon, even though I was willing to let anyone in there kick me in the nuts if they could name a Blind Melon song that wasn't *No Rain*. The fact that that thing was printed and framed, coupled with the complete lack of any mention of the loss of Malcolm Young, did nothing to quell the Wrath bubbling in my guts like an Italian sub whose salami had been way past its prime and sell-by date. There was a sign on the door reading *No Shirt, No Shoes, No Fascism, No Service*, which made me wonder if Fascists were welcome here, if not outright required? There was a sign reading *CAPITALISM* under a big red bar sinister, ironically—God, I fucking hope it was ironically—placed right next to the equally absurdly priced price list.

I gazed over the undulating sea of man buns and white-girl dreadlocks. I just wanted to give my barber and my straight razor a hug and tell them how much I valued their presence in my life.

I wish we'd gone to Waffle House

Switch laughed at my obvious discomfort. "You're dying inside, aren't you?"

"I want to so open my veins in the bathroom so one of these shitheads would have to find me and clean it up."

Switch grimaced. "Nick, just don't ask anyone in here about the bathroom."

Well, that was the verbal challenge that stood as the equivalent of "don't look down." Anyone worth their salt should have figured what was going to happen next.

The place was cramped and crowded to the point that there wasn't any trouble or going out of anyone's way to nudge someone. So, I did. "Hey, where's the men's room?"

I not only stopped paying attention but actively started ignoring the hippy after the phrase "doesn't conform to the fascist binary gender-conformative, hetero-normative paradigm."

I glowered at Switch, who just laughed and slapped the table. "Told you so."

I sat back as far as I could and crossed my arms across my chest. "Why the fuck are we here?"

"It's the highest-rated coffee shop in town," Switch offered as if that was a consolation.

"That's because regular people don't rate things. They're too busy having fucking jobs and lives and shit." I gestured at the hippy hipster purgatory I was stuck in. "These fuck heads rate things because they're narcissistic enough to think they fucking matter."

It was at this point black-and pink-striped hair nose-ring girl at the next table decided to interject leaning in between me and Switch. She spoke with the lolling languidity of the pseudo-intellectual and self-important. "I would appreciate it..."

I couldn't take it so I just interrupted. "Yeah, well, I would appreciate it if you'd shut your suck and mind your own goddamn business. If I wanted your opinion I'd cram my hand up your ass and work your jaw like a puppet, you Fraggle-haired nosy piece of shit."

"Why, I never..." she gasped.

"Had a job where you paid taxes?" Switch offered with a smile.

"Had an enema that wasn't farm-to-table fresh organic *quinoa*?" I leaned close enough to her that she could feel my toothpaste brush across her skin on my breath. "Turn back to your fucking table or I'm going to take your lunch money."

As she turned back to her table Switch and I looked back to ours and saw a lady in a pseudo-vintage-looking hat and some pro-vegetarian T-shirt that didn't warrant reading had sat in our empty chair and pulled out a Steno pad and a pen, like we were about to be interviewed.

"Hello," she said so cheerfully at that time of morning that I wanted her to spontaneously combust.

"Sorry, ma'am." I tried honey this time. "We're saving that seat for our friend."

She pouted annoyingly and pointed to a sign. I looked and read, *NO SAVING SEATS, ENJOY EXPANDING YOUR AND OUR COMMUNITIES.* "Sorry," she said, obviously not sorry at all.

"Young lady..." She was somewhere in her early twenties so Switch wasn't inaccurate in that. "Can you just take my word for it that my friend here—" Switch gestured to me, "and myself if I had to could get rude and vulgar enough that you wouldn't want to sit here? Our friend is getting our coffee and she'll be here any second."

The young lady frowned and said in a lecturing tone. "The spirit of Astra-Mugs is about expanding horizons and making new friends." She sat her pen down and held out her hand. "I'm Charlotte."

"Charlotte, it's a pleasure, really. But seriously, we really need that seat for our friend."

Charlotte made no move to budge. She smiled insipidly. "Tell me about yourselves."

I sighed and looked to Switch. With a resigned nod, he half-whispered, half-moaned, "Go ahead."

I reached over and grabbed Charlotte's hand squeezing it harder than she was probably used to as I shook it, not letting go.

"Charlotte, if you could have a sound effect happen when a man orgasms, what would it be?"

She tried to pull her hand away but I wouldn't let her and just kept shaking it up and down. Her eyes wide with confusion. "What?"

"See for me," I smiled inanely, "I'd kinda want a comically wet fart sound." I pushed air into my cheek and let it slowly bubble out my tight held upper lip. "What about you Switch?"

Without missing a step Switch leaned into the table almost close enough for his beard to brush it, incidentally putting his face at level with the intrusive Charlotte's chest. "I think I'd rather just have an explosion of glitter."

"Lights or physical glitter?" I smiled, eyes locked on Charlotte's shocked face.

"Real glitter that would have to be cleaned up."

I got closer to Charlotte's face, still squeezing her hand. "Don't you think it'd be great if in porn, every time there's a money shot you heard..." I ripped the wet fart sound from my upper lip.

"Nick, I'm not sure she knows what a money shot is," Switch suggested.

My jaw dropped aghast. "Charlotte, do you not know what the money shot is? It's in an erotic film when the man completes. Usually on a face." I stared intently at the bridge of her nose and made the wet fart sound again as I rolled my eyes up then sighed.

"Charlotte," I said, smiling, "do you think the Indians got a raw deal?"

"Native Americans," Switch politely corrected.

"So so sorry, Native Americans." I gripped her hand tighter causing her to wince. "Do you think the Native Americans got a raw deal, Charlotte?"

She winced and stared at her hand in my grip, but she nodded.

"They shouldn't have gotten encroached on should they?"

She shook her head. "Please, let go of my hand..."

I leaned close, forcing my forehead to hers. Close enough that her eyes looked like one big eye in my vision. "If they got a raw deal and encroachment is wrong... get the fuck off our table. Because you're as welcome here as smallpox."

I didn't let her hand go as much as I threw it back at her. She stumbled to her feet almost knocking the chair over. It wobbled from leg to leg before finally settling down.

I sat back and looked to Switch and we both started laughing. We drew stares and we didn't care.

Gretchen walked up with two disposable mugs with lids and cozies. "What's funny?"

"Your man and his people skills." Switch chuckled as he took his mug and took a sip.

Gretchen smiled before blowing over the small hole in the lid then taking a sip of hers.

I've never been a coffee drinker myself. I have known too many people who useless as shit till they had their first cup of coffee, and I had just decided I'd rather be useless all goddamned day.

Gretchen looked at me as I glanced around. "Nick, you okay?"

"I want a meteor to hit this fucking place." I sighed as I leaned forward crossing my forearms on the table.

"So," Switch said trying to be more helpful than my tired brain felt like trying to be, "do we have anything resembling a plan?"

"Go, get shit faced, pass out, let the world end?" I offered.

"Well, if that's the plan I'm going to skip the drinking and find some companionship." Switch chuckled.

Gretchen pressed on even as the hipsters and assholes pressed in around us, bumping our chairs as they moved past. "So, why is Uriel trying to force things?"

"She's got nothing to lose." I pulled my flask out and started unscrewing the cap. "Everything's pointed to the world ending one day. So, from her point of view, why wait?"

"But shouldn't God be giving the orders?" Switch asked.

I shook my head, "Lucifer seems to paint it as if the Father has just been kinda watching since the beginning."

"Okay," Switch offered, trying to be helpful. "I don't want to be that guy, but, and no offense, Nick, can we really trust Lucifer?"

"He's always seemed to shoot us straight." Gretchen said slowly, defending Lucifer but definitely thinking about it.

"Armageddon happens, Lucifer's stuck in Hell forever. And the little imp fucker didn't seem to relish that idea. So if anyone has a reason to draw things out, besides us, it's Lucifer." I didn't want to think of the idea of Uncle Lew not really being on my side. Maybe it was naive, but if he'd not been shooting me straight, I was ready for the world to come to an end. "I don't think the Fiery Sword is powerful enough to stop either side, but it's powerful enough to make them pause. But neither side trusts me, and that's one of the big problems."

Gretchen sipped her coffee and reached out to squeeze my hand. "We're fighting for a status quo, and neither side believes that."

"We got no one that can help us that we can ask shit. Lucifer's hands are tied, Gabrielle isn't necessarily in the loop. It's fucked." I sighed, but I squeezed Gretchen's hand.

"Too bad we don't have an oracle or anything," Switch sighed as he scratched his beard.

"What about a prophet?" Gretchen asked.

Switch and my eyes shot to hers. "Yeah," I offered, "that might fucking do."

"You know an honest-to-God prophet?" Switch squeezed his coffee mug hard enough to make the top pop off.

"Well, no," Gretchen admitted. "But I know where one happens to live."

"Okay?" I asked.

She lowered her eyes sheepishly. "You're not going to like it."

Switch started working the lid back on his coffee. "What else is new?"

Chapter Twenty-One

Prophet or Net
"Modern Love" David Bowie

I instantly hated the idea. The only thing I hated more was that I couldn't think of anything better, which meant I was stuck with Gretchen's bad idea. That in and of itself was confusing. She was usually a good idea machine, pumping them out the way Spacely's pumped out sprockets. I didn't hate the idea because it was dangerous, I hated it because it felt like a waste of time. Yet here we were, seven-and-a-half hours from the end of the world, standing in the front of an assisted living center.

The girl working the desk was wearing pink, but not clothes that looked like they should be pink. She was dressed like a serious, professional grown-up. The cut and style of everything should have been what someone with a laser pointer in a boardroom should have worn but instead, it was pink like a serious person's clothes had been in a Bismol explosion. The flowers on her lapel were pink, her shirt was pink, her jacket was pink, her glasses rims were pink, and I was willing to bet the pink cape thing hanging on the coat rack nearby was hers, too. She was in her late twenties but dressed like a secretary in a 1940s coloring book where the kid coloring it had just gotten lazy.

That said, I couldn't tell you what she looked like, but what I could tell you was this woman was seriously pink. In all honesty, she'd have done great as a bank robber. *I dunno, officer...I just remember pink.*

I stepped up to the desk. Gretchen was with me, wearing a white lab coat complete with pocket-protector that she lifted from the costume bin at Sharky's. Her hair was tied back and she was wearing a pair of rectangle tortoise-shell glasses.

The girl at the desk looked up and was about to open her pink lipstick-smeared mouth when I held up a hand and said, "Ma'am, I'm Dr. Carter McCoy. This is Carol..." gesturing to Gretchen. "We're here to see Ms. Ripley."

She looked down and leafed through some pages on a clipboard. "I don't have anything here about a visitor for Mr. Caulfield. I also don't have any Dr. McCoy on the list of approved physicians." Her face then broke into a grin. "Doc McCoy, like *Star Trek.*"

I vomited a little in my mouth but choked it back down. "Yep, he's my grandfather, or was, God bless him." I hated when people fucked up references. I also hated *Star Trek*. Give me the corporate dystopia of *Blade Runner* any day over that communist utopian crap.

I reached in the inside right pocket of my jacket and pulled out my fake police credentials. I flashed them with a practiced hand, letting my suit jacket fall open enough to show the underarm rig. "Doctor as in psychiatrist with the police department. It's nothing major, but we think Ms. Ripley can give us some insight on some things."

Her smug confidence, bolstered by the backing of paperwork evaporated with the flash of a police badge. She pulled out a binder and opened it to a page with a log-in sheet. I smiled. "Is that really necessary?"

She blanched and then blushed, shaking her head with embarrassment. "Sorry, offi—er, doctor, go on in."

I looked at the board of room numbers and found *Ripley, E.* We headed down the hallway Gretchen a step to my left and a step behind that I didn't really like. I preferred her next to me, not this odd subservient shit. But appearances had to be maintained I guess, and to be honest she was better at playing this kind of thing than I was. So if that was the way she was playing it I'd roll with it.

I put the back of my hand to my mouth and yawned. Then I dug my knuckle in my eye before shaking my head and yawning again even less politely.

I felt Gretchen prod me in my ribs and I realized I had walked past the door. I stopped and came back to it. I took the chart out of the holder by the door and lazily flipped through it while nodding. It seemed a "doctor" kind of thing to do. I looked at the name and sighed, feeling myself lose even more faith in humanity.

I stepped inside and let Gretchen slide past me before I shut the door. I felt myself glaring at the lady in the bed. She could have been writing out the cure for cancer and I would have still disliked her. "Seriously?" I asked. She looked toward me but her eyes had that milky glaze that belayed the fact that she couldn't see shit. "Ellen Ripley?"

She smiled the grin of a child who is standing with their hand in the cookie jar when their parents ask *what are you doing?* Her head cocked a little to the side presenting a little more ear as she heard us. "One name's as good as another, isn't it?" she asked so not-quite-petulantly that it definitely came out petulant.

"What's your real name?" I leaned back against the door. Gretchen glided over by the window.

"Ellen Ripley." She stuck to that story.

"Fine, well, I'm Dwayne Hicks and that's Newt." I gestured toward Gretchen. It was out of habit; I knew the lady couldn't see what I was doing.

"Why am I *Newt*?" Gretchen asked with a slightly annoyed purse to her lips. "Why not Vasquez?"

"Because we really should put you in charge," I offered with a shrug and was rewarded with a smile.

She did a little curtsy.

"So, what's your real name?" I asked the lady in the bed. She had that odd-looking age on a lady that I can never figure out how old she is. I wouldn't have been surprised to find out she was in her forties; I wouldn't have been surprised to find out she was in her sixties. Sometimes you just can't tell, or I can't anyway.

Which is also an odd juxtaposition because my Jailbait or No Meter is calibrated with the perfect accuracy of predicting a third-world election where only one candidate is running because the others committed suicide by shooting themselves in the back or throwing themselves off balconies.

"What do you want?" the lady asked. Her voice sounded like she'd sang lead for a metal band for years while working for a second job chewing up coal to shit diamonds for industrial drill bits.

I gestured to Gretchen, again out of habit—I wasn't intentionally trying to fuck with a blind person. "My friend here says you're your a prophet."

"F-I or P-H-E?" she asked.

"*Fa* not *Fi*," Gretchen said as she sat on a rolling stool that was in the corner. She smiled with childlike glee and gave herself a spin on it.

"And how would you know?" the lady asked. I refused to think of her as the heroine of the *Alien* franchise.

"Trust me," I assured her. "She knows weird shit."

"Like what?" The lady asked cocking her ear toward Gretchen.

Gretchen chewed her lip then offered, "The first movie to ever show a toilet flushed was Alfred Hitchcock's *Psycho*, 1960."

The lady clasped her hands together on top of the covers as she sat up on the bed. "That's obscure, but not really odd."

"Point being," I interjected, "we know you're a freaking prophet."

"So, what do you need a prophet for?" she asked.

"Shouldn't you know that?" Gretchen responded. "I mean, you're supposed to be the eleventh best prophet in the world."

"Eleventh?" I asked her. "It's the end of the damned world, probably, and we couldn't even crack the top fucking ten?"

"Oh," the blind woman said, "that's today?"

"Shouldn't you fucking know that?" I felt a little bad at yelling at a blind woman. If she had some Matt Murdock shit going on that might have been painful for her. Yet she seemed nonplused. "What kind of fucking prophet are you?"

"What do you think a prophet is?" She seemed bemused and that was annoying.

"See the future and stuff?" Gretchen asked, which was curious because this was her plan—shouldn't she already have a better grasp on crap?

The blind lady shook her head. "No, God talks to us directly, that's it."

"What do you mean *directly*?"

"Normally, he sends Gabriel to deliver his messages." The lady reached up and scratched her head and made her hair go even crazier than it already was.

"Gabrielle," I corrected.

"What?" she asked curiously.

"Never mind. So, God talks to you, so what?" I checked the clock; it was already after lunch.

"Well," she offered with an annoyed Socratic air, "why do you assume he says anything often? Or useful for that matter?"

"How often do you chat?" I asked, leaning back against the door. I didn't think anyone would try to interrupt, but I wasn't risking it either. Fucking hospital-style doors without locks.

"Three times." She smiled, very proudly.

"Three times a day?" Gretchen asked brightly.

"Total." The lady nodded annoyed that we weren't getting it. In our defense,

I was getting it, I just didn't like it. "Three times in your whole freaking life?"

She nodded.

"What did he say?" Gretchen asked; there was no hiding the wonder in her voice.

"Well, first, he started giving lottery numbers but then apologized for talking to the wrong person. So I only got three numbers, not really enough to win anything."

"That's a bummer," I offered consolingly.

"The second," she pressed on, "he gave me the secret to making the perfect omelet. He said you use two eggs not three..."

I interrupted her. "So, you're telling me God is L.L. Cool J from *Deep Blue Sea*?"

She thought for a moment. "I don't think I've ever seen that. Is it a movie?"

I admit that I was tired, I was annoyed, I was getting exasperated. "Lady, you're fucking blind. I don't know that you've ever seen anything!"

She chuckled. "I guess that's true."

"What's the third thing?" Gretchen pressed on. At least she was on task.

"Oh, about six months ago he said to come off my diet and start eating pudding again because the world was probably about to end, give or take anyway."

Gretchen's eyes met mine; we'd both instantly done the math in our head. That was about the time all this started with the Fiery Sword. Gretchen then looked back to the profitless prophet. "What's he sound like?"

"British," she didn't even hesitate. She had had that answer right there in the chamber. "But not like posh British, like, regular British."

"So not James Bond British but *Young Ones* British?" Gretchen asked with the intensity of an investigator about to solve a crime.

"I don't know what that is," the prophet admitted.

"Which one?" Gretchen pressed, "James Bond or the *Young Ones*?"

"Does it really matter?" I asked.

Gretchen chewed the corner of her lip then sadly shook her head.

I looked at the lady in the bed. "Well, thanks for nothing."

"If the world doesn't end I'm coming back for the omelet recipe," Gretchen told her.

"Well, wait," the lady offered. "Just because he didn't tell me doesn't mean I don't know stuff. Prophets talk. We have a party line."

"Seriously?" I asked, my hand on the door handle. "Those things still exist?"

"Have you heard anything?" Gretchen asked the far more pertinent question.

The blind lady nodded. "The prophet—like the head prophet on the world right now, the one God talks to most—he said the world's going to end, it can't be stopped, but it could be delayed."

"How?" I asked because delayed was better than five hours from now.

"He didn't say specifics, but he said it was up to Tommy and Gina." The lady nodded adamantly, patting the back of one hand into the palm of the other as she said the names.

"Who are Tommy and Gina?" Gretchen asked.

The lady sighed. "I was kind of hoping you two were Tommy and Gina, who it's said would never back down."

I felt my jaw drop and I looked to Gretchen then I looked to the more or less useless prophet. "That's Bon Jovi."

"Huh?" she asked.

"That's *Livin' On A Prayer* by Bon Jovi," I said slowly like I was explaining to a child that chocolate milk doesn't come from brown cows. Even though that was silly and there was no science to

support that chocolate milk didn't come from brown cows...
Goddamn I needed sleep.

"Oh." The lady smiled. "So you've heard the prophecy?"

"The fuck?"

Chapter Twenty Two

Take My Hand, We'll Make It I Swear
"Livin' on a Prayer" Bon Jovi

S o Gretchen and I found ourselves sitting down at the side of the blind lady, who kept insisting her name was Ellen Ripley. Part of me wanted to just brush her claim off as bullshit, but at the same time, it was one of those things that seemed so stupid it had to be true, because who could make up something that stupid? It was the narwhal of stories, proof of the validity of creation because something that stupid had to be made; it couldn't just happen.

"So, you're telling me," I asked with absolutely no credulity, "you've never heard *Livin' On A Prayer*?"

Gretchen's jaw fell slack as she looked at me. "That's what you are taking issue with here?"

I nodded. "Hell yeah, everything else is so batshit stupid that it isn't worth thinking about. But not having heard *Livin' On A Prayer*?

I'm willing to bet you can go talk to the freaking clicking people in Africa and they've heard *Livin' On A Prayer.*"

"Clicking people?" Gretchen looked confused.

"Yeah," I nodded, "the folks that talk with all pops and clicks and shit."

"The Koysan peoples," the crazy lady in the bed offered.

"Don't help him," Gretchen told her before continuing with a much more civil tone. "So, you're telling us that the rockstar Jon Bon Jovi is the world's greatest prophet?"

The lady nodded. "See, most of the time God sends messengers, but those messages can get all skewed. That's where prophets come in—we get the straight dope."

"What do you mean *messages get all skewed*?" I asked as I leaned back and crossed my arms, doing everything I could to look skeptical of a lady who couldn't see me anyway.

"Well, the way the prophets talk about it, Gabriel took a bunch of messages to Mohammad. Your basic *Be Excellent To Each Other/Party On, Dude* stuff. Problem is, he got the messages while hanging out in a cave that had natural gas deposits, so he was high as a kite. So *Be Excellent To Each Other/Party On, Dude* turned into *It's cool to toss homosexuals off buildings* and *It's fine to rape nine-year-olds as long as you get a guy to say you're married first.* You know, skewed." She leaned her head back for a few moments like she was looking at the ceiling, but I was pretty sure she was still blind. "It's like when kids play that game where you whisper something and it goes around, but because it gets screwed up the message ends up different?"

"Okay?"

"So..." She slowly waved her hand like she was unconsciously directing an orchestra that was not in time with the tempo of her talking. "God talks directly to some prophets. Problem is you end up telling someone God talked to you you end up whacked out on anti-psychotics and locked up in places where you have padded walls and no shoelaces. So, your average prophet nowadays comes in two varieties: crazies and creative types."

"Isn't that redundant?" Gretchen asked with such a profound earnestness that I realized she wasn't being sarcastic, but if she were trying to be sarcastic it would have been perfect.

"Maybe a bit." The lady smiled sheepishly.

"So, you're saying," Gretchen was verbally trying to work the logic out, "Bon Jovi's success is because he's putting out the direct word of God?"

"No," the lady shook her head making her hair flail like cilia. "Pretty much everything gets interpreted, explained, expounded, edited, *et cetera*."

"Tommy and Gina," I prodded, "tell us about Tommy and Gina."

"The Prophet," she began.

"Bon Jovi," Gretchen said a little too dreamily.

The lady nodded, "Bon Jovi said on the party line that the world ends, that can't be stopped. But that makes sense, doesn't it? Everything that begins has to have an end. I mean even if God didn't just call the game, sooner or way later, you know, energy death of the universe or something like that."

She sat there. A good minute passed and I realized she was looking for some kind of response. I looked to Gretchen and she shrugged. "Okay." It was lame, but it was what I had to offer up. I was tired and the world was ending in as many hours and I had fingers one of my dick-beaters.

"Well," she continued, "Jon said we couldn't stop that. It's as inevitable as corrupt politicians or rambling stories told by a toddler. But he said he was told that there were two who might be able to delay things. He called them Tommy and Gina."

I chuckled.

Gretchen shot me a concerned look then groaned. "You're about to speak only in Bon Jovi quotes now, aren't you?"

I shrugged.

The prophet continued. "He didn't say how. He just said if anyone could delay it, it would be Tommy and Gina."

"Well," Gretchen asked, "did he say anything about Tommy and Gina?"

She shrugged. "Tommy would be a pretty basic guy, Gina would be living under her potential."

Gretchen laughed.

The prophet pressed on. "He said they'd never have PhDs but that might be what saved us?"

"How?" Gretchen leaned in with her elbows on her knees and her knuckles under her chin.

"He said Tommy's a doer, not a thinker, and Gina would have his back. So maybe it's just in the doing, not the thinking?" The lady in the bed bowed her chin. "We don't know, it's just supposition."

"*It's hard to hold on,*" I offered, "*when there's no one to lean on.*"

"Don't do that," scowled Gretchen, seeing through my fun. "So, what do we do?"

The prophet shook her head. "I don't know." She paused, sitting there silently before asking, plaintively, "So, it's today?"

"Yes." Gretchen didn't sugar coat it at all.

"What are you going to do?" the prophet asked quietly, with worry. You could feel her concern, at the same time you knew it wasn't for Gretchen and me.

"*You live for the fight when that's all that you got,*" I offered.

"Seriously," the prophet asked, "what do you plan on doing?"

I sat there for a moment. I looked at Gretchen. Her dark eyes and mine found each other with the familiarity of magnets. There was a concern in Gretchen's eyes, too, but it was different than the concern coming off the prophet. The prophet, "Ellen Ripley" was concerned for herself and what was coming. Gretchen's silent concern was for something more. To Gretchen, it didn't matter what happened to us. You could see it in her eyes as clear as the stars on a cloudless night. She was fine going out like Jammer as long as the world was here tomorrow.

I loved her for it and I hated her for it. I would have liked it more if I knew when the shit started flying, that she'd run. That'd be easier for me to live with. But she wouldn't. She would go with me, as Jammer once put it, *dick-deep in stupid*. I'd have liked her more if I knew she'd run. I loved her because she wouldn't.

"What do you plan on doing?" the prophet repeated with a shake in her voice.

I smiled, eyes never leaving Gretchen's. *"I'm going down in a Blaze of Glory."*

Gretchen smiled, and I felt better for it.

I knew we were done here so I stood. Holding my hand out to Gretchen, and with a cocky smirk, I sang softly, *"Take my hand, we'll make it I swear."*

She laughed and shook her head. But she took my hand and I pulled her to her feet. I kept pulling and tugged her into my arms. I was tired, but I wasn't so tired I couldn't hold her.

"That feels nice," she whispered into my lapel.

"Your love is like bad medicine." I smiled into her hair.

She looked up and mock hit me. "Hey!"

I smirked. *"Bad medicine is what I need."*

"Okay, you need to quit that." She said it, she probably meant it, but she laughed. That made it worth it.

"You two need to get a room," the prophet muttered.

I thought about it for a moment; she might have been right. If the world was going to end anyway there were definitely worse ways to go than tangled up with Gretchen. Our eyes locked and she cocked an eyebrow. She was thinking the same thing.

It did get me thinking. And for more than a minute, I pondered taking a dose of Fuck-It-All and just letting the world end. We live in a world where the shit you work hard to earn gets taxed when you leave it to your loved ones when you die. A world where parents leaving babies to cook to death in cars isn't news but is bandied about the news nonetheless. A world of banned books. A world where what to do about female genital mutilation is something whose solutions are discussed, ignoring the obvious answer of shooting the cock bags who do it in the fucking face. A world where people sue people who sold them coffee for the coffee being hot when they spill it on themselves. A world where athletes and entertainers are mistaken for being important. A world run by whack jobs because they're the ones making enough noise to get noticed and the reasonable people get drowned out, or are smart enough to never play that game to start with. A world where people are afraid of science and science gets bent to politics. A world where *Firefly* got a truncated season, *Farscape* canceled on a cliffhanger, and yet the Kardashians pop up every goddamned day. A world where I still didn't have a goddamned jet pack even though sci-fi writers, TV, and moviemakers had been promising me one forever. A world some dumbasses still thought was flat. A world where more people would recognize the cast of *Jersey Shore* than could tell you who Edmond Hillary was or the amazing shit he did. A world that had yet to give me a World War Two-through-X-1-flight-years Chuck Yeager biopic.

A world that didn't have heroes anymore because, honestly, it didn't fucking deserve any.

A world that could go fuck itself for all I cared.

I hated most people. I didn't know the rest, which meant I didn't care.

You can't blame a guy for thinking, just for a moment, "Let the world fucking burn." We could find the nearest hotel, get a room and spend the rest of the world destroying everything in it in a fuck frenzy.

Then I thought about the handful of people I did care about. God knows there weren't many of them.

Six months ago I would have said *fuck it* and gone, found a place, copped a squat with Jammer, and attempt to end as many bottles of Scotch I could before the world ended. The Scotch part still didn't seem like a bad idea.

But there were a handful of people who deserved better. People who, despite all evidence to the futility of it, tried to make shit better. A handful of people who deserved more than what any demon or archangel wanted them to have. A handful of people who looked at the world and instead of saying *fuck it* would say *fuck it* then would continue keeping on keeping on.

I owed them because they'd never failed me.

I felt the corners of my lips tug up into a smirk. Gretchen gave me an adoring, even if it was questioning, look.

"What are you going to be today, Nick Decker?" She smiled and leaned up, and tugged at my lower lip with hers before whispering. "I'm fine either way."

I took her hand and we walked to the door. I tugged the door open with the loud cracking sound you find with doors at medical establishments. Out in the hall we were met with the quiet cacophony of regular everyday people living their regular everyday humdrum lives unwitting to the fact that the world was going to end unless a jackass who really needed a drink, but didn't need to go to meetings because of it, could save it.

Not save it; it couldn't be saved. But it could be delayed.

"Are you going to answer her?" the prophet called from the bed.

I looked to Gretchen the back to the prophet. I felt Gretchen's hand in mine and I gave it a squeeze.

We couldn't save the world, but we could delay it. How? How could the two of us stop the two greatest armies in all creation from ripping the living shit out of themselves and taking our world with it?

Gretchen smiled, and I felt less tired. In fact, I didn't feel tired at all, but I did feel beat. There's a difference.

Even though I spoke to the prophet, my eyes were locked to Gretchen's, and the smile I couldn't keep off my face was for her as well.

"*I'm a cowboy, on a steel horse I ride. And I'm wanted, Dead or Alive.*" She kissed me. I held her tight. I whispered, "*I'll never give up the fight. I'll go the distance.*"

Chapter Twenty-Three

**If I Ever Leave This World Alive... Or Any Other Applicable Flogging
Molly Song
"If I Ever Leave This World Alive" Flogging Molly**

S witch waited outside in his truck. Gabrielle had hooked him up with a jacked-up modified Toyota Tundra. The damn thing had a snorkel and God knows what else. KC Halogen lamps on the roll bar; the interior had a roll cage. The tires were idiotically large, not monster truck large but still pretty ridiculous. The bed was basically non-existent due to truck boxes and other equipment storage devices. In all honesty as idiotic as I thought some of it was, that truck was probably perfect for his *I blow shit up for a living* business.

He was wearing clothes that actually belonged to him now instead of hand-me-down Jammer garb. Cargo slacks, a button-up flannel, and a gray jacket hiding his pistol on his hip. Sitting between the seats of the truck was a pump shotgun.

Switch had posted up outside just in case. That was the world we were living in now. *Just in case* wasn't a silly or paranoid thought anymore.

"Find out anything good?" he asked as he leaned back against the frame of the open truck door.

"Our coming was foretold by Bon Jovi." Gretchen smiled, and the smile did nothing but obviously confuse Switch even more.

"Okay," he said slowly, reaching up to scratch his beard. "Did we learn anything useful?"

I couldn't help but smile. Were it not for Switch's subcontinental background, he would have been the perfect World War Two British example of *Keep Calm and Keep Buggering On*. It reminded me Gary Oldman had finally gotten his Oscar for his portrayal of Winston Churchill. I wondered if Uncle Lew was pleased about that.

"The whack job in there," I said, gesturing back to the assisted living joint, "said we couldn't stop the end of the world, but we could delay it."

"That's vague," Switch complained. It wasn't helpful, but it was a lot more accurate than the whack job prophet we'd just talked to. "So, is there a plan?"

I nodded slowly. "Yeah, but it's not a good one."

"Are your plans ever good?" Gretchen asked.

"Hey!" I really needed her on my side, especially for what I was thinking.

"What do you have, Nick?" Switch asked as he rubbed his knuckles.

"We gotta limit variables. I ain't gonna be able to think of what to do if I gotta worry about everything. We got too many variables." I knew what the next move was, but I knew I had to build to it.

"Okay?" Switch nodded.

"First, I need you to go grab Megatron. Her *modus operandi* is to hunker down, I need you guys to run. Get her then get a burner phone from Agnes. When you do tell Agnes to scram as well. After that, I need you to go and crash in on my brother. I can't have shit going sideways because some immortal shit head tries to come after me at the last minute using my nieces and nephews to get the Sword."

"Nick…" Switch started, but I interrupted him.

"I need you to close out the variables, Switch." Then I looked at Gretchen. "Both of you."

Gretchen didn't just look offended, she looked hurt. Her eyes got wet. "No."

"Gretchen…" Switch said. God love him, he may not have liked it but he saw the logic of the plan. He may have hated it, but he saw what I was trying to do and was backing me. I wondered if civilians had friends the way veterans did?

"No," she stated adamantly. She glared at me with those shining, abysmally dark eyes. "It's like Jammer said, *if the situation were reversed you'd be right there with me, dick-deep in stupid.*" She reached out grabbing my face in her hands so there was nowhere for me to look but in her dark eyes. She brought our foreheads together. We were so close the focus shifted and it looked like she had one large eye instead of two. "This started with us, Nick. You and me, there at Sharky's. When the Heaven's Hotdogs came it was us. This started with you and me. That's how it's going to end."

The tip of my nose brushed hers. "Tommy and Gina, huh?"

I saw her cheeks rise as she smiled making her large, optical illusion eye narrow. "*We're halfway there.*"

I smiled and whispered, "*Livin' on a prayer.*"

She let go of my face and reached down taking my hands. I let go of her right hand with my left and slid my arm around her, pulling her into my chest. I looked to Switch over the top of her head.

Our eyes met and there wasn't anything to say that our slow, shallow nods didn't convey. Gretchen slid around to my side and I held out my right hand to Switch. I felt Gretchen squeeze my waist as Switch and I clasped forearms.

"I'd fight this with you." His voice was quiet, but quiet in the way that a steel sword knew it didn't need to be a brass bell.

"I know."

His fingers dug into my forearm. Then without a word Gretchen slid from my side with the silent grace of a moonlight shadow and slid her arms around his neck. I smiled as his beard bunched up on her shoulder and tangled slightly with her silken raven hair.

"You take care of our boy," he told her quietly, "because God knows he's a fuck up."

"I will," she assured him. I couldn't tell her expression as her face was buried and muffled in his shoulder.

They slowly extricated themselves and I did see Gretchen smile. "You try not to let Megatron drive you crazy."

He laughed and nodded. Then he turned to climb up in his lifted truck. He stopped before he pulled the door shut and looked back at me. "Strength and Honor, Nick."

I felt the smirk tug the corners of my lips. "Smoke me a kipper. I'll be back for breakfast."

"You know," he said with a surprisingly carefree smile, "I have never fucking known where you got that."

I felt Gretchen look up as I chuckled. "I got it from a Brit TV show called *Red Dwarf*."

"It action or something?" he asked with arched eyebrows.

Gretchen snickered and I smirked. "It's a comedy."

He silently chuckled and shook his head. "That's fucking fitting." He reached over and cranked the truck then looked to me. "See you in Hell, Nick Decker."

I smirked and nodded as he shut the door.

Gretchen and I stood in silence as he drove away. There was nothing really to say till he was out of sight, and even then we stood arm in arm, silent but for our breathing.

"That was a good thing you did," she said quietly, eyes still on the road where Switch's truck had disappeared.

"Broken watch is right twice a day." It wasn't a lot, but it was what I had to offer.

"So how do you think this is gonna end?" I felt her turn her eyes to me. I kept looking down the road; I wasn't sure how I'd react when I looked at her. I could see myself being fine, and I could see my damned knees falling out from under me. Oddly enough neither of the options seemed like a great outcome all things considering.

I reached into my jacket pocket and pulled out my flask. I gave it a shake and knew it was about three-quarters full. I slowly got the top off and took a slow swig. I let the Scotch sit cool in my mouth and felt it slowly getting warm. I swallowed before it lost its appeal. I slowly started screwing the lid back in place. "I think the world's gonna fucking end. But the good news is we're probably gonna be dead before that happens." I slid the flask back into my pocket. I glanced at her, our eyes meeting. My knees didn't give out. "So, three cheers for little victories, I guess."

She smiled, but a sad one. "I couldn't go with him."

"I know." I reached up and brushed some of her hair back behind her ear. She leaned her cheek into my fingers. "But you know I had to fucking try."

"I know." I watched her mouth as she spoke. I could think of worse people to spend the last few hours of the world with. "So what now?"

I took her hand and we started walking to the car. "We could stop by, talk to a few cops, see if anything odd's on their radar. You feel like putting a call into the Sisters in Shadow? See if they have any fucking idea?"

"Not really," she admitted. "But if that's where we're at I'll suck it up."

We walked back across the parking lot toward the back of the building where we parked the Ferrari. That wasn't a security thing but more a *the fuck I want my door dinged by a Chevy Impala or Jeep Grand Cherokee?* concern. That said we still scanned around the corners before taking them. Three-ish hours till the end of the world was no time to drop our guard, and Gretchen never questioned it.

Like I'd always said, "Paranoia: you only gotta be right once for it all to be worthwhile."

A back door opened, and Gretchen threw her long jacket open to get her hands on the grips of her pistols. My hand was under my jacket with the speed of lightning reflex to get my hand on the familiar wooden grips of my OD green Springfield 1911.

A skinny white dude came out the back door. Even wearing long sleeves you could tell he had full-sleeve tattoos. He carried two large, black trash bags over to a dumpster. He set one down and pushed open the sliding hatch on the dumpster's side and slung in the first bag.

So Gretchen and I had probably overreacted. Then again the day we were having, that kind of response was Pavlovian.

We laughed and to each other's hand and started walking again.

God, I was tired; I knew it and knew I probably looked it. Gretchen on the other hand looked as rested and chipper as I had ever seen her. There wasn't a lot to get annoyed about in regards to Gretchen, but that was definitely on the very, very short list.

"Are you even tired?" I asked her, the curiosity getting the better of me.

"Exhausted, how about you?" How could she answer that with a smile?

"I feel like I've been fucking beaten by baseball bats and bags of cats."

"Bags of cats?" she asked with obvious confusion.

I shook my head. "I'm so fucking tired that my simile well is drier than a thing that should be wet but is really, really dry at the moment."

"Coffee would help." She giggled, knowing my thoughts on coffee.

"Hot whore taint water." I chuckled and squeezed her hand.

"We're probably going to die today right?" she asked offhandedly.

"It's looking like it." I didn't see a point to lie, fib, obfuscate, or any other way to shade or aim the truth somewhere else. Didn't help that she could see through me like a recently cleaned window on a clear day.

"Well," she asked with a laugh, "if you die can I have the Ferrari?"

I shot her an incredulous look. "You can't fucking drive."

"What's that matter?" She smiled mischievously. "I could always sell it, then I'd be able to afford Ubers for life."

"Sure," I shook my head. "I die, you can have all my shit."

"Why, thank you." She smiled demurely. "A fancy car and what, twenty-three whole dollars?"

Sometimes an idea gnaws on you. Sometimes an idea brains you over the noggin like a baseball bat. This turned out to be the Pangalactic Gargle Blaster of ideas.

"Holy fucking shit!" I stopped in my tracks and my jaw fell.

"What?" Gretchen asked, scanning around us for danger before looking at me in confusion.

My eyes met hers. "I think I might know how to save the fuckin' world."

Chapter Twenty-Four

Archangels Drive Ducatis Apparently,
and The Heaven's Hotdogs are Still Obviously Douchebags
Any song from the Car Chase Mix

W e were sitting at the edge of the parking lot, poised to pull out on the road when we saw her. Red hair cascading down around her shoulders, pale skin, dark sunglasses that gave her an oddly insect-like look, red leather jacket, black very tight leather pants, and biker boots sitting atop a motorcycle. Apparently, archangels drove motorcycles.

"You see her?" Gretchen asked as she started scanning around us for other threats.

"Yeah, I got her," I said quietly, my eyes locked on Uriel.

Her wrist flexed and her bike revved. I didn't take my eyes off the archangel as I asked.,"Anything else?" I could hear other motorcycles, deeper and more guttural than the street bike the ginger terror sat atop of.

"Four guys on cruisers coming from the right," Gretchen said with her usual nonplused calm. "They're Heaven's Hotdogs."

I chuckled. "Think they're mad about what happened to the local chapter?"

Gretchen smiled. "Probably not pleased." She leaned forward and shrugged off her jacket then arched her back to get her pistols off her hips. I figured that was probably a good idea and pulled the 1911 from under my arm. Then I drug my two spare mags and set them under my right thigh so I could pull them quick.

I looked at Gretchen and smiled. Here we were again like we were back at the beginning even though this time we knew we were at the end. I stuck my 1911 under my left thigh and put my hand on the gear shift. Gretchen reached over and interlaced her fingers with mine on the knob. I rolled down our windows then put the car in gear.

"Shall we?" I asked with a smile fueled by the happiness of insane, desperate situations, and exhaustion.

Her smile was brighter than the Big Bang. "No time like the present."

I dropped the shifter into first and gave her some gas. There was no squeal of the tires as we rocketed out onto the road. Spinning the wheel left putting the bikers to our back. The engine roared with a fine-tuned precision as I glided the shifter through the standard H of first, second, third. I held it in third as I cut a turn wide, pulling us to the right and heading north on a non-median four-lane road.

Gretchen laughed. "You have the blues?"

"Huh?" I whipped us past a Volkswagen Jetta.

Gretchen motioned to a street sign with the barrel of her pistol as we tore past it. I barely made it out. It had read Hill Street.

"We got bikers parallel a block to the right," Gretchen calmly informed me.

I glanced as we tore through an intersection. "Uriel's a block to the left." I glanced at her. "Let's try to not fuck this car up like the Miata."

She laughed but nodded her agreement all the same.

"We got to get out of town but these guys can't follow us." I felt the anger start bubbling in my guts. The thought of these guys following us where we had to go, things they would try to do to people I care about. Goddamned these shit heads for putting me in this kind of situation.

I down geared and fishtailed us around a corner pulling to the right. I reached down and pulled up my 1911 into my left hand and held it out the window. Taking my eyes off the road as we roared through the intersection. We passed behind the group of four bikers who had been paralleling us.

I got one good shot off, but it was focused by the Wrath. The .45 ACP glided under the back of the biker's helmet and punched into the base of his skull. It traveled with a slight upward angle blowing out the bridge of the man's nose and causing his left eye to explode in its socket. Gretchen was sitting up on the door sill aiming up over the roof of the car. She fanned off four quick shots with her revolver. I don't know what happened to the other three, but at least one punched a biker in the shoulder causing him to slump over his handlebars. That knocked them askew at an angle that wasn't quite conducive to the forward momentum and caused the bike to tumble, crushing and skidding the shot rider with it.

I got my hand back inside and we lost sight of the rest of them as we were through the intersection. I heard Gretchen slowly cook off her last two shots, aiming behind us, before she slid back into her seat and started reloading her custom six-shooter.

I glanced in the mirror and saw a chunk blown off of Uriel's small Plexiglass screen.

"Fuck beans, she's closing fast," I muttered.

Gretchen leaned so she could look out the properly adjusted side mirror on her side. "That's a Ducati 1199 Panigale R."

"Okay?"I managed to eek the car between a Fort Taurus and a Kia Sorento without touching either.

"Well," she smiled as she tossed a handful of empty brass out the window, "at twelve-hundred cubic-centimeters and packing a hundred and ninety-five horsepower, that thing, I think, is the fastest production bike in the world."

"How fucking lovely," I grumbled, glancing back in the mirror. "How the fuck do you know that?"

She shrugged. "It's not that weird a fact. Same as knowing the Hennessy Venom F5 has a claimed top speed of three hundred and one miles per hour. Rocking a seven-point-four-liter twin-turbo V8 rocking a cool sixteen-hundred horsepower making it the fastest production car in the world."

"When did you become a damned car commercial?" I grumbled as I wove between the juxtaposition of an Audi and a garbage truck.

"You're one to talk, *Mister I Know Weird Shit*." She actually took the time to stick her tongue out.

"Well, Uriel's keeping up." I wasn't happy about it but denying it wouldn't fix it either.

"Well, at least she knows her shit," Gretchen said sliding shells into her revolver's cylinder with grudging respect.

"Oh, she just Googled it," I offered with a smart-ass grin.

Gretchen kept loading, but the way she sucked her lips before smacking them gave away the fact that she was actually thinking about it. "Do you think archangels Google?"

"I dunno." I glanced ahead and saw a bit of clear road. I checked the rearview and saw that at least two other bikers had joined her. "Take the wheel and keep her steady."

I didn't even wait on her to acknowledge. I leaned my upper torso out the window and aimed my 1911 behind us in my right hand. I took a second, focused the Wrath, and aimed. Eight-round magazine, seven rounds left. I pressed off two rounds for each of the bikers and then the remaining three at the archangel.

The first biker was bent low over his handlebars so for all I know the rounds went down his gob and out his ass; regardless he went over like a Jenga tower. The second biker found himself with a spreading red stain blooming on his white shirt under his vest, and he too went over, hard; adding insult to injury he slammed into the back of a van. Uriel, much to my annoyance, Darth Vader'd all three rounds into the palm of her hand with little more than a grimace.

I slid my arms and head back in the car, dropping the spent 1911 into my lap. Gretchen grabbed the pistol and one of my spare mags from under my right thigh and started reloading it for me.

"Gretchen, sweetie..." I glanced in the mirror before looking forward to dart, with squealing tires, around a delivery truck.

"Wait," she asked as she dropped the spent mag and ramming the fresh one home before thumbing the slide release, "are you officially pet-naming me *Sweetie,* or is that a facetious thing?'

"Which would you prefer?" I tore through a red light and saw a Honda plow into an unknown parked car.

Gretchen slowly lowered the hammer then reached over pushing it between my legs and under my left thigh. "I'm good either way."

"Well, either way, you mind reaching back and pulling out those HK UMP45s that are back there?'

"Crap, I forgot about those!" She sounded excited as she leaned back between the seats and opened the case. I flipped a left, taking us parallel along the interstate cutting over road. I remembered the valve clattering mess of my old Miata, and no matter how much I loved that car I appreciated the sheer *works really well* of the Ferrari that wasn't on its last legs.

I dodged past the lady pushing the stroller close enough to flip her skirt up high enough to expose her very not-stereotypical mom panties. Gretchen was too busy ramming stick magazines into the submachine guns to notice.

Up ahead I saw five bikers pull onto the road, and instead of driving, they were pulling into blocking positions just beyond an exit ramp. I checked the mirror and saw Uriel coming up behind us on the traffic-weaving Ducati.

Gretchen flopped back in the seat and her eyes went wide. She grabbed her seat belt and tugged it over her lap as I reached over grabbing one of the UMP45s. I held it like a pistol as the folding stock was collapsed to the side. I took it in my left hand; we were about a hundred yards short of the bikers. Luckily they hadn't started shooting yet seeing as they were armed with various pistols.

I rammed my foot down on the clutch and spun the wheel. The car squealed and skidded and rotated. I kept my right hand on the wheel and aimed the sub-machine gun out the window with a straight left arm.

We slid and skidded past the exit ramp and started coming to a stop thirty yards short of the biker makeshift barricade. Behind me, I heard Gretchen cooking off clean three-round bursts from the UMP45. I grabbed the Wrath and let it steady me. I knew the HK had a twenty-five round stick mag. We were still spinning to a skidded stop as I got aim on the first and opened fire with the fully auto option. I could never have done it without the Wrath. But I took down all five bikers with the cyclic magazine. Cordite smoke rose from the end of the barrel as I scanned to make sure I didn't need to come up with the 1911 to finish anyone off.

"Now, you can show 'em your badge!" I yelled, remembering the line from the movie.

Gretchen laughed.

I looked across to her and out her window as I pulled my arm back inside. Gretchen's gunfire had caused the archangel to angle off onto another block and out of our line of sight.

I dropped the sub-machine gun on my lap and got us in gear. I fishtailed the car as I pulled us up the wrong way of the exit ramp. We were going almost seventy by the time we got to the top and I slammed the clutch and brakes, spinning the wheel. We twirled twice before I got us straightened out and heading the right way down the interstate.

Gretchen grabbed the sub-machine gun off my lap and started reloading it with a spare magazine from the box in the back. Then she reloaded her own as I checked the mirror making sure we were clear.

"I told you you were more Mike Lowery than you thought." She smiled as she put both safeties on.

"I still say I'm not cool enough to be Will Smith." So far we were clear behind.

"Probably not," she agreed. She sat the reloaded HK back in my lap, barrel facing out. "But you'll do."

I glanced at her and batted my eyelashes like a blushing debutante. She laughed; that made it worth it.

With the sub-machine guns out Gretchen arched her back again and put her six-shooters in her holsters. I figured it was a good idea and slid my 1911 back into my underarm rig. I put my one spare magazine away then reached over to the glove compartment and pulled out a freshly loaded one, putting that under my right arm as well. So even if we had to run from the car I was combat-loaded.

Gretchen took a box of .357 rounds from the glove compartment and started pushing shells into the empty slots on her pistol belt.

I checked the mirrors and hazarded a glance as we sped down the interstate. So far we were still clear.

"Dang it," Gretchen sighed as she put everything away in the glove compartment and shut it.

"What?" I asked, glancing around trying to see whatever it was she'd have noticed.

The disappointment was palpable in her voice that bordered on anguished. "We forgot to turn on the Car Chase Mix."

Chapter Twenty-Five

...FOR THE WIN!
"Supercharger Heaven" White Zombie

It should have taken at least an hour to get out there. But in a Ferrari that you know is never going to get pulled over by the cops I cut that time in half. As we pulled out of town we got the windows up because the helicopter noise of the windows down as we flew down the road was annoying. I stuck the HK UMP in between the door and the seat and it wasn't a discomfort.

Things were getting worse.

It wasn't just the exhaustion trying to drag my eyelids shut or the subtle throbbing behind my forehead. I would feel the Wrath roiling in my guts. Gretchen sat half-backward in her seat staring behind us. I glanced back in the mirror, risking it even at the breakneck speed I was hurling us down the interstate. I couldn't see if Uriel was following, but I knew she was there. I don't know how I knew but I knew.

"What do you think it is?" Gretchen asked quietly. She was usually pretty unflappable but not now. She was worried and I couldn't blame her. Things were starting to snowball even if I didn't know exactly what was going on. The sky was clear, but that didn't stop what looked like lightning ground strikes from flashing throughout the city behind us.

"I got a guess but it's nothing reassuring." That was as close as I got to reassuring. A handful of hours before the final battle and vague had become the closest thing to comfort I could provide. I reached up and rubbed the bridge of my nose and the corners of my eyes. I was damned tired. I could remember when I'd woken, but for the life of me, my brain had stopped functioning at a point where I could process the math to calculate how long ago that was.

"That's them gathering?" she asked.

I nodded and edged around a semi-truck. The driver had no idea that the odds that his cargo would ever get to where it was going was slim to shit. "I'm guessing so."

"Do you have a plan, Nick?" Gretchen turned her large, liquid, and eternally dark eyes to me.

I met them and tried to memorize every detail. If I was going to cast into Hell for trying to stop the end of the fucking world, I might as well do it with as many details of Gretchen in my head as I could.

Because, I figured anyway, that was the point, wasn't it? There was the big story and the small story. Any asshole who said he was trying to save the world for the world's sake, in my opinion, was at worst a lying piece of shit; at best they were a damned moron.

Hemingway said, "The world is a fine place and worth fighting for" in the classic *For Whom The Bell Tolls*. I think the only way he was right was dependent on your definition of "the world."

Most people don't matter. They exist just as cells in the organism of greater humanity. At best they live, reproduce, and die. At worst they turn cancerous and fuck up bits of the metaphor. If the time I spent in Iraq and Afghanistan taught me anything it's that some men's only purpose is to deserve to get killed. Some people's only real purpose seemed to be existing just to be put down.

Most people didn't do a damned thing for the world. Some made the world worse. Some made the world better by what they brought to it. Some, me maybe, made the world better by what we took out of it.

The faux lightning strikes kept flashing behind us as we drove out of the city. I took my phone and punched in a text message that was either going to be the most brilliant thing I ever cooked up, or the world was going to end in a handful of hours. I figured there wasn't going to be a lot of middle ground today.

Gretchen glanced at me curiously but she left the obvious question unasked.

I knew Uriel was after us and I knew I couldn't lead her to anyone she could use against me as collateral. That was what sucked. If she were just coming after me that would be one thing. An enemy you could trust to come after you was something you could respect. I didn't trust Uriel to play the game fair. She already proved she'd come after me through the people I cared about. I couldn't let that happen again, even if I needed help.

It should have been an hour's drive out of town. I made it in less than half that in the Ferrari. We pulled off the interstate and whipped around the curves of back roads for another few minutes before I pulled over on the bridge over the gorge. A river I couldn't remember the name of flowed quietly several hundred feet down. It was a pretty view. You could see in the mountains where the deciduous oak forest transitioned into coniferous spruce-fir forest. It was a wild verdant Heaven/Hell-scape depending on your sensibilities.

"We never went camping," I said quietly as I looked over the view.

"I've never been camping," Gretchen confessed with the appropriate amount of shame for an admission like that.

"There's not a lot better than the combination of a campfire, cool night, and a flask of Scotch." I smiled over to her.

She arched her eyebrows. "Oh? What is?"

I shrugged. "The view of your wing tattoos as you got your arms out wide while you're bouncing on..."

She punched my arm. "Jerk." But she smiled.

In the quiet, I heard the sound of the Ducati engine before we saw her come around the bend and onto the bridge. Gretchen and I walked back to the Ferrari and took up our HK UMPs. She extended the folding stock and held it professionally to her shoulder. But the Spear of Destiny was already extended and laid strategically atop her left foot with a nearly perfect balance.

I kept the stock closed and held it like a giant pistol in my left hand. I felt the rage welling and I let it flow into my right hand. The Fiery Sword slowly emerged in my grip. This time it appeared as a smoothly curved katana, but too short to be a traditional katana. It took me a minute to recognize it as the blade of Juan Sanchez Villa-Lobos Ramirez, the sword from *Highlander*.

Gretchen smiled approvingly. "Nice."

"Just works out sometimes." If Uriel was about to kill me, going down with Gretchen's eyes in my mind wasn't that bad.

"You know, if that sword was supposed to be fifteen-hundred years old, how come the ivory in the handle wasn't yellowed all to crap?" she asked as Uriel began to slow before us.

"Not now, Gretchen," I chided her softly as Uriel pulled to a stop about twenty-five feet short of the two of us.

It was a very non-dramatic stop. She lowered the kickstand and slung her leg over the side. She wasn't wearing a helmet, but her hair was pulled back in such tight a bun that it might as well have been a helmet. Her boots, with a very impractical six-inch heel, clicked with each slow, molasses-like step toward us.

"I am here," she slowly informed us, "for the Father's Wrath." Her eyes flickered over the Spear laying nearly balanced on Gretchen's combat boot. "I'll take that as well."

"Lady," I said—God I sounded annoyed and tired. "We're here for shit that has fuck and all to do with you. So just make life easy, hop on your little toy bike, and scram."

She lethargically drew her long, thin rapier from thin air. It reminded me of the sword Inigo Montoya used to fight the six-fingered man, but nowhere near as pretty. But maybe that was because it was about to be aimed at Gretchen and me.

She started stepping forward; when she was about ten feet away Gretchen asked, "Now?"

"Yeah." So, the commonly given definition of insanity is doing the same shit over and over and expecting different outcomes. I'd emptied an entire mag of 10mm at full auto into Zadkiel and it'd done the sum total of fuck and all. Dunno why we thought it would be different this time, but Gretchen and I gave it the old college try.

Our HK UMPs loosed gouts of flame as we sprayed cones of hot copper jacketed lead into the torso of the ginger archangel. Uriel staggered a bit, then continued forward. There were holes all over her red leather jacket, but that seemed to be the extent of the damage. Even in the horrific realization that we were probably about to die and the simple sheer exhaustion that was weighing on me, it couldn't be denied that shooting firearms full auto was fun.

I dropped my sub-machine gun and lunged forward slashing with the Fiery Katana. Uriel sidestepped me and slashed. My momentum carried me past her and I barely got around to block her rapier slash with my Katana. The good news was this put the annoying and powerful ginger between Gretchen and me.

I saw Uriel grimace as I heard the sound of rapid-fire .357 rounds. Gretchen was behind her, six-shooter in hand fanning the hammer. I didn't slash but thrust. As the last round punched into the back of the archangel's shoulders she barely turned my Blade. But she didn't turn it enough. The Blade ripped through her jacket and cut a gash into her upper arm. Instead of blood, light sprayed from the wound.

Uriel reached out with her wounded arm and grabbed me by the collar and slung me. My feet came off the ground and I went a couple of feet through the air before hitting the ground. I heard the slower, more aimed fire of Gretchen's second six-shooter, but that didn't stop Uriel from dropping her knees over my shoulders and dropping onto my chest. One of her idiotic heels pinning my right wrist down made the most powerful weapon in the universe impotent. Her rapier transformed into the type of dagger you'd expect a wack job Aztec priest to use to hack someone's heart out, except, you know, made of freaking light.

I knew that life, what little left there was going to be of it, was going to suck.

She screamed and raised the dagger high in both hands, ignoring Gretchen off to the side. I saw the horror in Gretchen's eyes. I probably should have said something before then, probably should have said something then, but hindsight's twenty-twenty, right?

Then I heard the tires screech and a blue Nissan Rogue slide to a halt next to Uriel and me, the open passenger side window facing us. She looked over just in time for the barrel of the Remington 870 pump shotgun to poke out the open window. She was close enough that the gout of flame from the end of the barrel smacked her in the gob as the light field game load slammed into her face. Even as the roar of the shotgun echoed in my ear Uriel fell from where she was squatting on me and bumped into the railing of the bridge.

I watched as Gretchen kicked the Spear up into her hands and spin it, slamming the shaft into Uriel's shoulders. As Gretchen drew it back the blade cut into the jacket, leaving a long slice that bled light. Uriel tried to get her dagger around but couldn't before Gretchen stabbed. The Spear of Destiny punched into Uriel's side under her left arm. Light sprayed as bright and rapid as a strobe light a psychopath would use to try and kill a group of epileptic kids.

Gretchen leaned into the shaft and pushed the large Spear tip deeper into the wound. Uriel screamed; light burned from her eyes, her mouth, her ears. Gretchen screamed as she drove the Spear deeper.

Then, Uriel exploded in a flash.

Gretchen, having leaned hard on the shaft of the Spear, fell, barely bracing and catching herself on her forearms.

Where Uriel had been now just sat a spinning ring of gold. The halo spun like a coin before finally wobbling and doing its best impression of a hula hoop coming to rest.

I pulled myself to my feet then reached down for Gretchen. Her hand felt good in mine as I pulled her to her feet.

I smiled and slid my arm around Gretchen, giving her a squeeze. I heard the car door behind me, the engine still running, and I turned my head seeing the towhead of a man standing as he cradled his shotgun in his hands and a very concerned look on his face.

Even with the anxious look, he sounded as unflappably calm as he always did. "Tell me I didn't just shoot some lady in the face for no good reason."

As exhausted as I was, I couldn't help but laugh. Gretchen did, too, then looked up with a beaming smile and laughed. "Phil the Destroyer for the win!"

Chapter Twenty-Six

Streets of Fire...
"Bat Outta Hell" Meatloaf

O ur business with Phil didn't last too terribly long. That was because the legal request wasn't too terribly complicated and because Phil was an amazingly thorough and professional dude. The longest bit was the ever-present speech *I'm not your lawyer, you're not paying me, this advice isn't sanctioned by any authority, this isn't my field, blah blah blah*. And even though he said all that, he still gave me the advice I needed and the help I had to have. That's the guy that Phil the Destroyer was. A guy who would tell you to turn yourself into the cops, but then tell you how to steal his car and give you a twenty-four-hour head start with the cops.

He gave me the envelope I needed, and then Gretchen and I followed him to a nondescript shotgun house occupied by Jeanette Fitzgerald, her husband Lloyd, and their son Curtis. Jeanette and Lloyd were both in their eighties; Curtis was in his fifties and had never lived anywhere but his parents' basement. Jeanette was sweet, grandmotherly, and wore a floral print dress and 1950s librarian glasses. Lloyd was the old-man skinny that came with once having been built like a Greek statue but weathered by age. His slacks were well pressed and his collared polo shirt was obviously thirty years old, but obviously well mended. There was a dignity to Jeanette and Lloyd. Curtis was just a piece of shit.

Phil laid the papers out on Jeanette's dining room table. I signed them, Lloyd and Curtis witnessed them, and Phil signed off as the person who prepared it. Then Jeanette came in with her stamp and pen and notarized it all. There were three copies in all. I folded one up and put it in a letter envelope and slid it in the flask pocket of my jacket with the flask. I gave the second to Gretchen. The third I gave to Phil.

I hugged Jeanette, shook hands with Lloyd, and ignored Curtis before Gretchen, Phil and I stepped outside.

"I'm not real sure what's going on here, Nick. And that," Phil said gesturing to my pocket, "doesn't make a lot of sense."

"Will it stand up in court?" I asked with all seriousness.

Phil nodded. "Where the law can apply, yes."

"Then it will do." I held out my hand and we shook. "Give my best to the girls, okay? And do me a favor, go slap happy with treats today."

"Okay?" he asked with raised eyebrows.

"It doesn't make a lot of sense," I said.

"It sounds certifiably crazy," smiled Gretchen.

"But the world might end in the next hour and a half," I finished, proving Gretchen right.

Phil studied the two of us for a second. "Well," he said slowly, "if it doesn't end we should get dinner tomorrow."

I couldn't help but smile. Gretchen's matched mine. That was Phil the Destroyer in a nutshell. Unflappable, calm, and positive. He was a guy who would have looked at the Great Flood as a simple yet interesting engineering problem. This was a guy who went to church on Sunday but saw the world for what it was: no worse and no better. Most people were shit, but then there were Phil and Tessa and their kids.

I hugged him. A guy who heard the world was ending didn't question, still planned for tomorrow, and kept on keeping on. I've never deserved friends with that amount of quality.

Gretchen and I parted ways with Phil and climbed back in the Ferrari. I started driving back into town. We kept seeing the flashes from the sky. They were coming with more intensity and regularity now. Yet no one else seemed to be noticing. It seemed like one of those things people would pull over to the side of the road to watch, but no one was. Maybe Gretchen and I noticed because we'd been around enough weird shit we'd become immune to the filter that got tossed over reality?

"Are you planning what I think you're planning?" Gretchen asked quietly as 102.9 FM Panther Radio, the *REAL ROCK*, played in the background. It was the beginning of Iron Maiden's *Run To The Hills*, which at the moment didn't seem like very bad advice.

But I told her it didn't take long because it wasn't a complicated or great plan. Gambit might have been a better definition. I told her my thought process and her idiotically important part in it. We were pulling back into the city as I looked over into her dark eyes. "So, whatcha think?"

Gretchen smiled, but it wasn't a particularly happy one. "I've heard worse plans, I guess."

"Oh, yeah?" I asked as I yawned into the back of my sleeve. "Such as?"

"You could be going to have a sledgehammer fight with Raven Shaddock," she offered.

"Yeah," I said with a sigh, then, "but you're too hot to be McCoy and you're too badass to be Ellen Aim so that simile kinda falls apart, doesn't it?"

A laugh escaped her lips. "Yeah, you're cooler than Michael Paré in a duster and a Marlin 30-30."

I chuckled. "Tonight is what it means to be young, I reckon."

She reached up and pushed her raven waves back behind her ears. "I don't feel particularly young right now."

"Add sixteen years and two war zones to that and you know what I'm sucking up right now."

Her cheeks lifted as she smiled. "Well, you wear it well."

"Fucking liar."

She laughed. More flashes scarred the sky. "This is really happening, isn't it?" Her voice was soft. I heard the fear there, but it didn't rule her. It was the fear I felt every time I'd stepped out the door to do my job as a Paratrooper, counting to four as I fell from a high-performance aircraft, waiting for the opening shock of the parachute. Knowing if I got through *One Thousand, Two Thousand, Three Thousand, Four Thousand,* and didn't feel the opening shock of the opening chute, I had to pull my reserve. Knowing that if the reserve didn't work I had the rest of my life to fix it. She felt the fear, but it didn't rule her. It was something to be more proud of than not being afraid at all. It was the first time I'd ever really heard it in her voice. I loved her for it.

Gretchen reached behind the driver's seat and pulled out a bag she'd put there earlier. She set the bag on the floor between her ankles, then reached over and started pulling off my belt. I didn't stop her, but I did shoot her a confused look. As she started putting it back on me as I drove—I would shift to help her—she threaded on two, black leather double mag holders. Putting four Wilson Combat eight-round .45ACP mags on my hips, two to the left, and two to the right. She unbuckled me and tugged at my jacket and helped me get it off. Then she took off my underarm holster. She tugged the OD green Springfield 1911 from the holster and set it in her lap as she threw the rig behind the passenger seat. Some holstered the pistol in a rig she pulled out of the bag and helped me put back on. I now had my 1911 under my left arm and Jammer's nickel-plated Kimber 1911 under my right arm. I got my jacket back on and my seat belt buckled back in.

It definitely seemed like if I was going out Gretchen wanted me going out swinging. And if that's the way it was, I figured we might as well go all out. I started driving toward the storage place we'd inherited from Jammer.

As I drove Gretchen got changed right there in the passenger seat. It was distracting but who would mind? She changed into a gray tank top, black yoga pants, her pouch belt with pistol holsters, her jungle boots, and the half-jacket she wore the day we met. She shoved the empty bag back behind my seat as I pulled into the storage place. The gate code was 80085: BOOBS. The padlock on the rolling doors had the combination 6969; I shouldn't have to explain that one.

Inside there were weapons placed up on pegs on the walls. I took down the M-60 and loaded it with a four hundred-round belt and fed the dangling excess into a satchel. Gretchen took down the AA-12 and loaded a twenty-round drum of double-ought buckshot. She then pulled down the sawed-off, pistol-gripped double-barrel shotgun she'd carried when we'd visited Peaches, what felt like a lifetime ago. She loaded it with shells from a box of Dragons Breath that set on a workbench. Instead of loading the weapons into the Ferrari, I took the keys off another peg.

Sitting there in the storage space was the coolest thing Jammer had ever owned, legal or illegal. A black van with a red stripe and spoiler. He'd juiced the engine with nitrous oxide and he'd lined the interior with Kevlar sheets that would at least stop most pistol rounds. He'd never used it because no situation had ever felt "cool enough" in his opinion. But it was the end of the world. So we started loading our weapons into Jammer's replica of the A-Team van.

Go big or go home, right? Dick-deep in stupid.

"You know, this is all well and good," Gretchen said warily, "but we still don't know where? I mean, we can't just make the rounds of the parks hoping."

I nodded, knowing she was right but not knowing what to do about it. I walked to the Ferrari and hopped in. Gretchen slowly pulled out the A-Team van with the caution of a driver who had little idea what she was doing and I pulled the Ferrari into the storage spot. I took the HK UMPs with a few fresh mags and tossed them in the van, too, before locking the storage space.

The annoying thing was that it felt like I knew. Like when you know *the name of the movie with the guy about the thing* but just couldn't remember it at the moment. I climbed behind the wheel of the van. Jammer had it set up with not just GPS but with a full internet-capable computer system, like what you'd see in a cop car but just connected to the internet.

"Do me a favor," I said quietly. I felt a thread and started tugging on it with my mind. "Pull up a city map."

Gretchen started clacking at the keyboard. "Okay."

The Real Rock Station played, the DJ talking how there were reports of riots starting to break out in the city. I turned up the volume and listened, but it made sense. I figured even if the populace couldn't see the flash of teleporting angels and demons there had to be some kind of psychic bleed. The animal part of the brain reacting to the coming calamity?

"Got it," Gretchen said as she looked up from the screen.

"Okay." I bit my lip. "Can you pull up the original city plan and overlay it?"

Gretchen nodded and started tapping away at the keys. "Gimme a second."

After reporting about the growing number of riots, the rock station started playing Judas Priest's *Breaking the Law*—someone had a sense of humor or was just really oblivious to circumstance.

"Got it," Gretchen proclaimed and then turned the computer screen.

It hit me, and I really hoped I was wrong.

I let my fingers trace along the lines of the streets until they came together, right at the entrance of Memorial Park. I sighed. "It's there."

"You sure?" Gretchen's head was almost lying on my shoulder as she leaned over and looked at the map on the screen. But she hadn't gotten it yet.

"Yeah, I'm sure." I wished I was wrong, I wished the end of the world was more than an hour off. I was tired. Then again, either way, this was almost done.

I pointed to Veterans Avenue. "In the original city plans, this road was Megiddo"—I then pointed to Hill Street—"and this Blues-y route has always been Hill Street."

Gretchen smiled. "I see what you did there; that was cute."

"Thanks." She was focusing on the map but I was looking to her. "In all that crap Megatron gave us, the first page..."

Gretchen interrupted, "All you read was the first page, wasn't it?"

"Shut up." But she was right. "The first page broke the word down. Armageddon was really two words originally. It's Greek from *Har*, meaning hill." I tapped Hill Street. "And Megiddo, some place in Israel." I tapped Veterans Avenue, Megiddo on the original city plan. I put my finger to Memorial Park, setting at the corner of Hill and Megiddo. I looked away from the screen. Gretchen turned the screen to study it more intently.

"Gretchen, Armageddon isn't a damned event." I put the weapon loaded A-Team van in gear with a fatalistic determination. "It's a mother fucking address."

Chapter Twenty-Seven

*SHUT THE FUCK UP, JEREMY BENTHAM, I'M BUSY DOING ANTI-
HERO SHIT!*
"Shoot to Thrill" AC/DC

It would have been really nice if we could have just gotten on Hill Street or Veterans and just taken it to the entrance of Memorial Park. But the stupid rioters made us take a route that, on a map, would have looked like it had been drawn in crayon by a drunken preschooler whose art would go on the refrigerator door to prove mommy loves them and not because it had any artistic merit.

The radio kept putting out news updates about the riots and their spread in between playing songs that were probably inappropriate due to the circumstances.

"This is bad, isn't it?" Gretchen asked, cradling the AA-12 in her lap.

"It's not good," I admitted as I pulled through an alley to get off the road.

"This the time to come clean about everything?" she asked, her head facing away as she looked out the window, not that she needed to, but to avoid eye contact.

"Come clean about what?"

"There are things you don't know about me," she confessed.

"Hit me then."

She bit her lip and even with her olive complexion, you could tell she was blushing. "My favorite musician is Dolly Parton and my favorite actress is Sally Field, but I hate *Steel Magnolias*—I tried to make myself like it but I just couldn't." She looked at me apologetically, lip quivering. "I just couldn't."

I couldn't help but smile. "I'm not gonna bitch. I hate that movie."

She wiped a tear from her eye. "Dylan McDermont deserved better."

"After *Hamburger Hill,* hell yes he did." I reached over and took her hand in mine. I squeezed it and she wiped her other eye with her free hand. "It's not that big a deal."

"I just felt like I was hiding something from you is all."

I pulled onto a road that ran parallel to Hill; so far, it looked relatively clear. "I hate Barry Manilow, but I love the Me First and the Gimmie Gimmie's version of *Mandy*."

"That's not that bad." She smiled. "I got thrown out of a performance of *The Phantom of the Opera*."

"Why?"

She sucked on her lips then bashfully confessed, "I stood up and yelled at the stage."

"What the hell did you yell?"

"I'd rather not say."

I laughed. "Well, now you have to."

She waited, the embarrassment growing before finally sprouting, "You dumb bitch, he gave you everything."

I laughed; she slowly smiled. Then I told her, "I hate musicals."

"That's not shocking." She squeezed my hand this time. "I like working at Sharky's because I don't feel like I have to work as hard as I would if I worked at Titanium Lightning."

I laughed even more.

"What?" she asked with a voice filled with concern.

"I'm probably not supposed to find laziness attractive."

She smiled, and that made it all worth it.

The closer we got to the park the weirder things got. It wasn't just rioting. Sure, there were plenty of people looting, plenty of people fighting. But there was also odder stuff. There were people just outright fucking there in public. There were whole orgies taking place on the hoods of cars that were not built or engineered for those kinds of stresses. There was a swarm of people latched to an abandoned hot dog cart like iron filings to a magnet, just gorging themselves. I saw two women fighting over a jacket they were both trying to pull off a shop dummy; one of the ladies literally shanked the other with a nail file and that still didn't stop the other lady from trying to win that ugly ass jacket.

We passed the scene of a sorority-looking girl finger banging herself while watching a dude in a clerical collar going to town all mouth happy on easily the largest piece of meat I'd seen outside a porno.

"This all seem a bit odd to you?" Gretchen asked with understated curiosity.

"A bit," I admitted.

A group of raged-out assholes ran up and started banging on the van, blocking the road. I grabbed one of the modified Glock 17s with the cool German sears and a thirty-two-round magazine in my right hand as my left hit the button to roll down the window. I pushed the pistol to the guy at the window's screaming face and squeezed the trigger. Five hollow point 9mm rounds barked in a blast of fully automatic fire blowing out the back of the man's head. I heard Gretchen firing what sounded like one of her single-action .357's from the other window. I switched the pistol to my left hand and aimed it out the window blasting a woman banging on the front of the van. At the same time, I punched the gas. The van bumped as it shot forward, and I didn't wonder if I ran anyone over but I did wonder how many people I ran over.

There was a little voice flirting with the back of my head telling me I should feel bad about that. But the voice of Jeremy Bentham screamed in my inner ear *You have bigger fucking things to worry about right now!*

"This is crazy," Gretchen said with glorious understatement as she started reloading her revolver.

"Maybe," I was totally guessing, "the End of the World is bringing out the crazy in people. Cranking all the suppressed shit up to eleven?"

"Maybe," she agreed as she slid the pistol back in the holster. "But why isn't it affecting us?"

I thought about it, and at the same time, I could feel the Wrath barely contained. It wanted to be unleashed. In that split second that occurs every time I blinked I saw myself, burning Blade in my hand giving the world its just desserts. Some of it was actually gratifying. Using the Fiery Sword to chop off the cock of every child molester. Taking the Burning Blade to behead every producer of reality TV and dismember the executives who canceled shows like *My Name Is Earl*, *Community*, and *Firefly* while shows like *Teen Mom* continued to pave the way for porno people who weren't talented enough for porno. I could see myself taking the unbridled Wrath of God and feeding the glutton, sating the lustful, working the slothful, satisfying the greedy, contending the envious, humbling the proud, and drowning the wrathful in more than they could possibly fucking imagine.

My knuckles were white on the steering wheel and I realized I was fighting to keep my shit together. "Maybe we're just used to the bullshit?" I offered.

Gretchen thought about it and didn't even seemed fazed at I swerved to miss a crack-head skinny guy going to town behind a rascal-riding tubby. In swerving, I did hit and run over an asshole who had been swinging a tire iron.

"Do you think the Sword is protecting you?" she asked.

"I dunno...I'll be honest I'm trying to not flip my shit right now." I glanced at her and saw the concern in her eyes. "Plus, that doesn't explain you being fine."

"You're okay," she offered, "and I am because of the soulmate thing?"

"Sounds good," I admitted as I gunned the engine and leaned half my head and left arm out the window, cooking off the rest of the full-auto Glock mag into a crowd of people fighting in the middle of the road. Some scattered, some fell, and some got slammed with a supped-up GMC Vandura doing damage to its grill. I pulled my arm back in and dropped the spent pistol into the floor between the seats. "Sounds good, but who fucking knows?"

"It's not like it matters." Gretchen nodded.

"Huh?"

She shrugged. "We're still relatively okay, even in all this." She gestured at the world falling apart. "The why of it all doesn't matter. I know gravity works; understanding the science of it is just masturbation."

We were within a block of the park entrance. I glanced at the clock—nine minutes till when the imp demon said the world was ending. The road was blocked with cars and people in a surreal hodgepodge of fighting and fucking.

I put the van in park and leaned back, grabbing the M-60 and slinging the heavy satchel with the belt over my shoulder. Gretchen slid the sawed-off double-barrel in the back of her belt and hefted the AA-12. Our eyes met. We didn't say anything.

If *the time comes* and you take the time to say all the things there is to say, the moment is going to pass. I unlatched the door and pushed it open with my foot and lead the way out the door with the barrel of the M-60.

My feet touched the ground and I saw a cop aim an obviously empty Beretta 92FS at me, and confusion crossed his rage twisted face when the gun wouldn't fire. Pointing an empty gun at me or not, I put six rounds into him, low into his hips and gut from the belt feed.

See, a lot of people practice and preach *two to the chest and one to the head.* But that's just silly. If you know your opponent might have body armor, two to the chest is silly. Then putting one in the head? The head is a target half as wide as the chest, so you double your chance of missing. The hips, on the other hand, are just as wide as the chest. They also have important veins running through them. And finally, you can't stand on a broken hip, so even if you don't kill the asshole he's off his feet. Those six 7.62 x 54 rounds all hit and basically folded that cop in half.

I started stepping toward the park. I stepped over a couple who had to be in their eighties laying in a disturbing sixty-nine. I brought the M-60 to my shoulder and sent a spray of brass as I raked a group of people lighting a car on fire. A guy wielding a bike chain spun it over his head and ran toward me in a mad rage, but Gretchen punished the dude with three shells of double-ought buck with finality.

Gretchen got beside me and we moved together.

There were at least fifty people, maybe more, between us and the entrance of the park. There wasn't time. It was like I could hear Jeremy Bentham whispering, *Your hands are tied, so fuck it, bro. Do what you gotta do.*

In a perfect world, we'd have worked our way around or used stealth to ease our way through. But we don't live in a perfect world, do we? My nieces and nephews were doing what kids do nowadays, Jammer's brother and sister were living their lives. Switch and Megatron were on the run. Yuri and Mary Jo were hiding at her sister's. Phil the Destroyer and Tessa were being great parents to their daughters and son. The world was going to end, and fifty people who may or may not have had it coming stood between us and the Hail Mary possibility of saving it.

I held the M-60 to my shoulder and pressed the trigger, cooking off rapid yet controlled bursts of three 7.62 rounds, five rounds then a tracer, over and over. I fired two or three aimed bursts with every slow methodical step. I dropped looters with the ease of stolen goods falling to the ground with a crash from their limp, lifeless arms. I put down people in the throws of passion for the simple combination of uncertainty and the sad fact that they were there. I gave a hell of jacketed lead to those who turned from attacking each other to try to attack us.

I'd like to say I felt bad about it, but I didn't. The sad fact is that *people* are statistics. The sad and glorious fact is I'd put down any number I had to for Phil the Destroyer and Tessa, for Yuri and Mary Jo, for my nieces and nephews, for Switch, Jammer, and every other brother I humped a ruck and crossed the wire with. I'd murder the world for Gretchen.

She matched me step for step, and when she emptied the drum of the AA-12 she dropped it and drew her pistols. Her shots were controlled and aimed and filled with pain. Tears fell down her cheeks and she obviously felt everything I didn't. I didn't envy her that, but I did love her for it. Not because she did it, but because she did it anyway.

Jeremy Bentham had said, *The said truth is that it is the greatest happiness of the greatest number that is the measure of right and wrong.* Gretchen and I put down at least fifty people to get to the entrance of the park. Just because someone in an instance is right doesn't mean they can't go fuck themselves.

We got to the gated entrance and I dropped the satchel of ammo and the M-60. Gretchen looked at me curiously as she started reloading her pistols. I pulled out my flask and unscrewed the top and took a long swig of eighteen-year-old Macallan. "You remember the plan?" I asked and offered her the flask.

She shook her head at the flask but muttered, "I do," as she holstered her first pistol and started reloading the second.

I gestured to the M-60 as I put my flask away. "Belt fed isn't going to save the world." I patted my pocket. "But this might."

She nodded, holstered her second pistol then wiped her eyes and cheeks. She made herself smile as she looked into my muddy brown eyes. She put her right hand in my left and squeezed.

Hand in hand we stepped through the gate into the park.

"I love you," she said softly with all the sincerity a man could ever hope to hear in the voice of an angel.

I Han Solo'd her.

Chapter Twenty-Eight

Michael Bay's Fourth Best Movie
"My Way" Frank Sinatra

...the end is here ....

It is without any hint of hyperbole or irony when I say Frank Sinatra had one of the greatest voices of all time. Even through the small speakers of my iPhone, there was no mistaking the tone and timbre of Ole Blue Eyes himself. I had asked Gretchen to pick a song, a song for the End.

When I say the End, again, it is without hyperbole or irony. The grass was soft and well-manicured under my sneakered feet. The wind was enough to tug at the edges of my jacket, exposing the pearl grips of the 1911 under my right arm and the wooden grips of the 1911 under my left. Even with the wind, it was a pleasant evening, and probably the last.

Frank sang about living a full life and all.

Gretchen stood next to me, and even here at the End she was a comfort. I wished she'd go but I knew she wouldn't. I was certain dying was easy. Dying was easy and dying fighting was *blood simple*. It would be so much easier if she weren't there.

But dang it, Frank did it his way.

Then again, it wasn't like she was safe elsewhere. This wasn't just a climax, it was the Climax. She would be no safer up on the International Space Station than she was right next to me. And at least here, she could die swinging. We could die together.

Frank may have had regrets, but doesn't everyone?

I wished Jammer and Switch were here. Switch was gone because I had sent him away, but he definitely would have had I called him. That's the damnation of having Brothers. Jammer was still dead.

Frank sang about doing what he had to do; preaching to the choir brother.

How many people had I killed since the entire shit show had been dumped on my lap? How many bodies had I stacked like cordwood in the name of putting off exactly what I found myself surrounded by?

Frank had a plan and did it his way.

Well, unlike Frank I couldn't say that about planning. Planning was never my strong suit. Maybe if it was we wouldn't have found ourselves here at the End of All Things.

Frank sang about being in over his head but sucking it up like a man.

Gretchen had to know.

Frank Sinatra sang of standing and bearing it.

That I had, though I'm not sure it was a virtue. I'm not sure anything was better. I wasn't sure anything could be worse. Hell on one side, Heaven on the other, and neither pleased to see us.

Frank sang about loving, laughing, crying.

I kind of wish I'd cried but I hadn't. I hadn't cried sober since I was eleven. I looked at Gretchen. The five-foot shaft topped with the Spear of Destiny clutched in her fists, more like a warrior goddess worthy of all the world's riches. She had to know. She had to know all the things I'd thought but never said. She had to know all the things I'd said that came out wrong. She had to know all the dreams I had about her, for us.

Frank had his share of losing.

Almost Switch... Jammer... Faith in Humanity... Faith in Heaven...Fear of Hell...

And yet, as he admits in the song, Frank was amused by it all.

To be honest I was struggling to find the humor.

Frank said screw being humble.

I smiled at Gretchen. She smiled back. Shy was never the style of either of us.

Ole Blue Eyes did it his way.

For good or ill, goddamned right we did.

Frank sang about the defining characteristics of a man, and what does a man possess.

Gretchen...

Frank sang about laying it all out on the table.

I looked to my left and saw Lucifer in all the glory of his Divine Birth, armored and decked out for war, a brace of three spears in his left hand, and a spiked Morningstar in his right. He stood surrounded by his Infernal Host in their dread damnation.

I looked to my right and there stood Michael, probably Rafael and Gabrielle bedecked as you'd imagine warriors of the Throne; Michael with sword and shield. Probably Rafael with a sword and ax, Gabrielle with a bow and arrows of light. The angelic armies arrayed in good order, prepared and ready for the Day that had come.

Like Rocky, Frank sang about taking the hits but moving through.

I looked at Gretchen. Our eyes touched for what might be the last time. She knew...she had to...

For the time had finally come upon us. Hell to the left, Heaven to the right. Gretchen and I in the center, standing at the End of All Things, upon the field of Armageddon.

Frank sang about doing it his way. *My Way* ended like the world was probably about to.

Goddamn my girl has great taste in music.

We approached hand in hand, and I honestly wouldn't have had it any other way. Well, maybe hand in hand with Gretchen and a company of Paratroopers at our back would have been nice, but all things considered, I was fine with things. But her hand felt good in mine, even as the faux lightning flashed.

We could see the armies gathering. One to our left and one to our right. I'm not sure which way the Father was facing so I couldn't tell you if the angels were on his right or not.

I was tired, but I'd settle for a drink. I pulled out my flask and got it open with my teeth so I didn't have to let go of Gretchen's hand. I took a swig and got it put away.

The armies stood to each side like a person who didn't know anything about the Civil War would imagine Civil War armies doing.

"Hope your plan works." Gretchen squeezed my hand.

I tried to smirk, but not sure at all I pulled it off in any shape, form, or fashion. "If not, I'll see you in Hell."

She laughed. What was the alternative at that point?

You could see all kinds of uniforms on both sides. Spartans from Thermopylae stood shoulder to shoulder with veterans of the Korengal Valley. A war of 1812 British Rifleman stood side by side with an irregular American Revolutionary guy with a Kentucky long rifle. Soldiers of both sides of any war I could name stood on the sides of both Heaven and Hell. Except Nazis. Oddly, all the Nazis seemed to be on Hell's side, with the notable exception of the *Fallschirmjager*, who were arrayed behind Michael with the other men who could be defined as Airborne. It was like someone wiped a rag over wet military history books then wrung it out over either side, here at the final battle.

My Way started playing on repeat and Gretchen said, surprisingly cheerfully—or with it being her, maybe it wasn't surprising at all. "We're a little outgunned here, huh?"

"A bit, yeah." I tried to smirk and didn't know if I succeeded in any shape form or fashion.

That's when I noticed a commotion on Heaven's side. A lone figure had broken ranks and was heading across the park field. Yet instead of heading toward the ranks of Hell, he was walking toward Gretchen and me.

He was armed with a Winchester lever-action saddle rifle like he'd been busy riding with Teddy Roosevelt in his cowboy days. On his hip he wore a G.I.-issue 1911 in the official World War One-looking leather flap holster. He had a sizable backpack on his shoulders with tourniquets rubber-banded to each strap. His hair was thick, but his beard was gone. Without it, there was no hiding the chin that couldn't be described as strong since the only word that fit was dominant. His tattoos were as fresh as they'd been the day the bandages had come off. He wore BDU bottoms, mirror-shined jungle boots, and his black shirt with a DL-44 wielding Han Solo and the caption *Han Shot First*.

Gretchen's eyes went saucer wide, and I couldn't keep the smile off my face.

"So," Jammer said with his easy, confident, self-assured smile. "Horatius-at-the-Bridge shit today, am I right?"

I couldn't help it. I threw my arms around him, crushing the rifle between us. I felt Gretchen try to get her arms around both of us. It was warm, fulfilling, and everything you'd want a hug to be.

Slowly, I dunno how long the hug lasted—seconds, years—we pulled apart. "Jammer." Gretchen reached up and wiped a tear away. "What are you doing?"

He nudged toward me with the butt of his rifle. "Dick-deep in stupid, right?"

I glanced at Michael then to Jammer. "I don't think they're going to take too kindly to, you know, I dunno, defection?"

Jammer just shrugged and slid his aid bag to the ground. "I've been in trouble before. So, is there a strategy or do you just plan on screaming *Chuck Yeager!* and attacking everyone?"

Gretchen laughed.

"No," Jammer told her. "He really did that when we came for you and he fought Zadkiel while I did the rest of the work."

I felt the smirk tug at my lips. I pulled out my flask and took another swig and offered it to Jammer. He took it and lifted it to his lips and gulped eighteen-year-old Macallan before handing me my flask back empty. I put the lid back on and just dropped it. If the world didn't end I could put it back in my pocket, and if it did end what was the point?

"There's a plan," I assured him.

"Cool." He looked to Gretchen. "So, what did you come up with?" She shook her head and pointed to me. Jammer's shoulder's slumped. "Well, shit."

"Hey!" If I sounded offended it's because I kinda was.

"Well," he said as he thumbed back the hammer on his rifle, "let's get to it. Waiting isn't going to make fucking this goat any easier or pleasant."

I nodded. "I'm glad you're here, both of you."

Gretchen smiled and Jammer nodded with a confident, "Wouldn't have missed it, Brother."

There was no way to avoid it and no time like the present. I looked down at my right hand and started thinking about the world ending. Gretchen being punished for her affiliation with me. Jammer getting kicked from Heaven for being the friend everyone should wish they had. I thought about the people I killed just to get here. I thought about Hollywood remaking movies that didn't need it. I thought about the *Star Wars* prequels.

I saw the short, leaf-shaped blade of the xiphos form as my fingers wrapped around the pommel. The blade made of fire, the very Wrath of God there in my grip. I could feel the rage roaring in me like a furnace that would have melted a Terminator, and Shadrack, Mishack, and Abbendego; I don't care how freaking protected they were. A fire looking to be unleashed, to punish the world. I was standing surprisingly still considering how hard I was fighting inside.

I grabbed the rage and forced it up, and unleashed it as I bellowed, "LUCIFER, MICHAEL, BAALBERIETH, GABRIELLE, AND BRUCE, GET THE FUCK OVER HERE!" The voice was mine, but it wasn't. It felt like I was a puppet dubbed poorly with the voice of God. Not the happy God, but the *Get in the boat, I'm about to drown the damned planet* God.

Everything was silent for the time being. The wind made no noise, the leaves weren't speaking up, the bugs decided this wasn't the time to be noticed. The armies of Heaven and the legions of Hell chose to be diplomatic and not make a peep.

Lucifer was the first to step forward; Michael was next. Michael stepped so fast it was obvious he wished he'd stepped off first and was ashamed he hadn't. Bruce and Gabrielle stepped off together and politely jogged to catch up with Michael. Baalberieth stepped off last and seemed in no hurry to get anywhere. Lucifer looked confident; Michael wasn't going to look less confident than Lucifer. Gabrielle and Bruce looked confused. Baalberieth looked like the kid who got called to the chalkboard and had no fucking clue what was going on or what to do when he got the piece of chalk in his hand.

I looked to Gretchen and Jammer and smirked. We all knew this was probably the end, and at least we were in good company.

There was no time for pleasantries as the others approached. Before they even stopped walking, Michael, with all the regal command the Champion of the Armies of Heaven could muster, proclaimed, "The time has come, it's time to pick a side, Decker."

"I'm afraid he's right, Nicholas," Lucifer agreed with a dour resignation.

I felt the smirk on my lips sit there easier. "Good, you two are agreeing. Let's keep that up while all of you shut your fucking sucks. I'm talking now, and you shit heads are going to listen."

This was the moment. This was the edge of the razor. This would decide if this world would have a tomorrow.

It was the moment I reached in my pocket and pulled out the envelope. I handed it to Baalberieth, the Archdemon of Lawyers. "Read it."

He took it and opened the envelope, drawing out the crisp, recently signed and notarized paper. I watched his eyes move over the lines of type and saw them become wide with disbelief. He read it again to make sure he got the gist, then read it a third time, letting the horror sink in.

He looked up at me, jaw slack, eyes filled with fear. "You dumb son of a bitch... do you know what you've done?"

I nodded. "I think so." My voice could have given liquid nitrogen freezer burn.

"Paper is meaningless at this point, Decker," Michael chided sadly.

"No," Baalberieth said in terror. "He's ended us all."

Baalberieth handed the paper to Lucifer, who read it far more calmly. At the end, he smiled and handed it across to Michael. Michael read while Gabrielle and Bruce leaned over his shoulders to read. Gabrielle covered her mouth as her jaw dropped.

"That's right, cock bags," I softly growled. I felt the Wrath tugging at me. It wanted to lash out at its disappointing children. You would think that would make me relate with my parents but it just made me madder. I held on, barely. "I wrote a fucking last will and testament, got it notarized and witnessed and everything. And in the event of my death"—I took time to glare into each and every one of their immortal eyes—"all my various weapons are left to my maternal grandfather."

It would have been an intimidating moment had Jammer not chuckled.

"So, I die," I continued, "and I'm betting that omnibenevolent Daddy is going to get really fucking abusive really fucking quick." I gestured between Lucifer and Michael. "Either of you fucks think the Father's gonna be pleased or understanding to either damned side?"

"Nick," Michael said slowly, like he was piecing it together as he went. "The Father separated the Wrath from himself for a reason."

"And after I'm kacked," I interrupted him, "the Father can give it away again, but he's going to have it for a little while. And I'm betting that little while is enough."

I would say silence filled the air, but it didn't.

"It's legal. It stands," Baalberieth quaked. "Decker dies and the Father..." He didn't finish the sentence, but even a limited imagination was enough to fill in the rest.

I pointed to Baalberieth and Michael. "You two are going to take the armies and go home. Right now."

Michael's eyes narrowed. "Or what?"

This was the moment. I heard the pistol fly from the leather holster, I felt the barrel with the sights filed away press to the point where my ear met my jaw and skull. I heard the hammer thumbed back. Gretchen, God love her, was about three pounds of pressure from killing me and sending the Wrath of God back to the Father.

I pulled Jammer's 1911 from under my right arm and thumbed back the hammer and pressed the barrel under my jaw as I locked eyes with Michael. I felt Jammer move to my right side, not wanting to be left out, and press the barrel of his rifle to my temple.

"You two," I repeated as I tried to bore a hole in the archangel Michael with my gaze, "take your armies and go home, or we end everything right... fucking... now..."

Baalberieth looked to Lucifer, and Lucifer didn't hesitate. "Do it."

Michael stepped back slowly, not wanting to turn his back on anyone. "Michael," I told him, "I'll see you at funerals, but that's it. Understand."

He nodded. "This ends nothing, it just delays something worse."

I nodded and felt the pistol under my chin even more acutely. I then glanced at Gabrielle and Lucifer. "We need to talk about how things are going to work now."

I slowly took the pistol from under my chin and I aimed it into the dirt as I lowered the hammer. I felt the barrel of Jammer's rifle pull away. Gretchen's pistol slowly pulled back from my skull. It was shaking as she did it. I was really glad she didn't accidentally shoot me.

In flashes of light and smoke, both armies started disappearing.

"Well," Jammer laughed, "I gotta go." He reached over and nudged my shoulder. "Good job, dummy." He hefted his aid bag and slung the lever-action rifle over his shoulder. "Later, gators." He then paused and looked to Gretchen. "Mind if I ask you something?"

She looked to him curiously. "Sure, hit me."

"What's your last name?"

I heard myself interrupt before she could answer. "Decker, if she wants it."

Jammer smiled, and Gretchen's eyes went wide. She stood there and shifted her feet from side to side. She bit her lip coyly. "That will do nicely."

I smiled, Lucifer and Gabrielle did, too.

Jammer turned and started to walk away until I called out, "Hey, Jammer."

He stopped and looked back.

I asked, "What's God look like?"

He smiled. "Michael Caine."

I smiled.

Then for the last time, he quoted the end of every *Cowboy Bebop* episode except *Real Folk Blues Part 2*. "See ya, Space Cowboy."

I nodded and quoted *Red Dwarf*. "Smoke me a kipper, I'll be back for breakfast."

Then, in a flash of light, he was gone.

Gretchen holstered her pistol and slid her right hand in my left. We both squeezed. I looked in her eyes and felt fine.

"So, what now?" asked Bruce awkwardly.

I finally looked away from Gretchen to Bruce. "Sorry, bro. Look, I'll be honest I called you over here because I knew your name."

"My name isn't Bruce," he tried interrupting.

I didn't acknowledge that. "So, really, you can jet, man."

Bruce didn't screw around. In a flash he was gone, leaving Gretchen and me alone with Lucifer and Gabrielle.

Lucifer broke the quiet with a polite and heartfelt "Congratulations" to Gretchen.

She seemed demure. "Thank you."

Gabrielle had a worried look on her face. "Nick, what you've done," she struggled to find the words, "it's so much worse than Armageddon."

"Nicholas," Lucifer added with forced calm. "Even if you live your life out without being killed in a random crime or car crash, how long do you think you're going to live with the way you take care of yourself?"

I looked at Gretchen. Then I looked to the devil and archangel. "So, this is how it's going to work. Once a month, the four of us will meet at Carl Paxton's Steak House, have dinner, and discuss business."

"And you guys will take turns paying," Gretchen added helpfully.

I nodded. "Yeah."

"And you're sending us on vacation," Gretchen half-laughed.

I looked at her. I couldn't hide the confusion.

She nodded. "We want two weeks, full butler package at Sandals Montego Bay."

I smiled. "Yeah, we're doing nothing but drinking all-inclusive booze."

"Eating all exclusive food," she added.

I smiled. "Scuba diving."

"And trying to break the bed and any other worthy surface." Gretchen smiled. I blushed at that one.

Gabrielle blushed, too.

"You've not saved the world, Nick," Gabrielle lamented softly, obviously not caught up in the insanity Gretchen and I were caught up in. "You've ended it far more horribly, just delayed what? Twenty or thirty years?"

"We saved the world today." Gretchen's eyes were shining and I was lost in them. It felt good.

I squeezed Gretchen's hand and finally looked away to Lucifer. "Uncle Lew, come on. You're telling me with magic Spears, Fiery Swords, and Bon Jovi, that there isn't some Fountain of fucking Youth? No magic golden calf we can stroke off to live forever? No Holy Grail? I mean even if we have to find the Ark of the Covenant first then some magic stones in India..."

"Temporal chronologically," Gretchen interjected, "*Temple of Doom* comes first, then *Raiders*, then *Last Crusade*."

"I'm just saying," I looked to Lucifer, "you're telling me there's not a loophole for eternal life or immortality or shit that she and I can exploit? Cause if we live forever, the Will isn't going to happen, is it?"

It is a simple fact. The best parts of my plans are the ones I make up on the spot.

Lucifer smiled.

About the Author

A veteran of the 82nd Airborne and a graduate of Auburn University, Dick Denny is a disappointment to his family, a fun guy to be around, and a handy guy to have about in a pinch.

More From From Foundations Books Publishing Company

What stands between humanity and the battle of Armageddon? A sword.

But not just any sword - the Fiery Sword that guarded the Gates of Eden after humanity was kicked out. Before the flood, it was stolen by the 23rd Demon kicked from heaven, who eventually married and imbued it into her human son. But now she'd dead, and it's starting to manifest.Humanity's only hope? Nick Decker, a scotch-swilling PI armed with a .45 and the Wrath of God, his nerdy ninja-stripper girlfriend Gretchen, and his loyal acid-dropping, street-doc, war-buddy Jammer.

When you do a job for Hell, Heaven expects the same.

When Archangel Gabrielle shows up at the door of Decker Investigations offering some kick-ass cars in exchange for a job, Nick takes it just to keep the peace. But finding the Spear of Destiny while dealing with the Teutonic Knight hit teams and Douchebag Demon Worshiping Academics is a tall order.

Good thing Nick and Jammer's old buddy Switch is in town.

Imprisoned for over a thousand years by the Diveneans of old, Lord Balthazar covets one thing: his freedom. Using his minion, Isafel, and an evil imp spawn called Ilio, they will search Etharia for the one thing that will set their master free and bring chaos to the lands—the Kruthos Key.With underlords scheming to take the throne and demons roaming freely throughout the land, it's a race against time. But one Divenean still lives, and with the help of an ex-General there may be hope left. But is it enough?

Sherman Lancaster has lived 119 years, and the only thing he fears is living 119 more.

Sherman's great-grandsons Piper and Sebastian are coming to stay with him, and they think it's because their mother can't afford daycare. But Sherman knows the truth: One of the boys will become his apprentice.

Sherman Lancaster lives by a simple code to which there are no exceptions:

The Guilty Must Pay.

Foundations Book Publishing

Copyright 2016 © Foundations Book Publications Licensing
Brandon, Mississippi 39047
All Rights Reserved

10-9-8-7-6-5-4-3-2-1

Abandon All Hope
Dick Denny
Copyright 2021 © Dick Denny
All Rights Reserved
ISBN-978-1-64583-040-5

Made in the USA
Coppell, TX
02 February 2021

49408569R00125